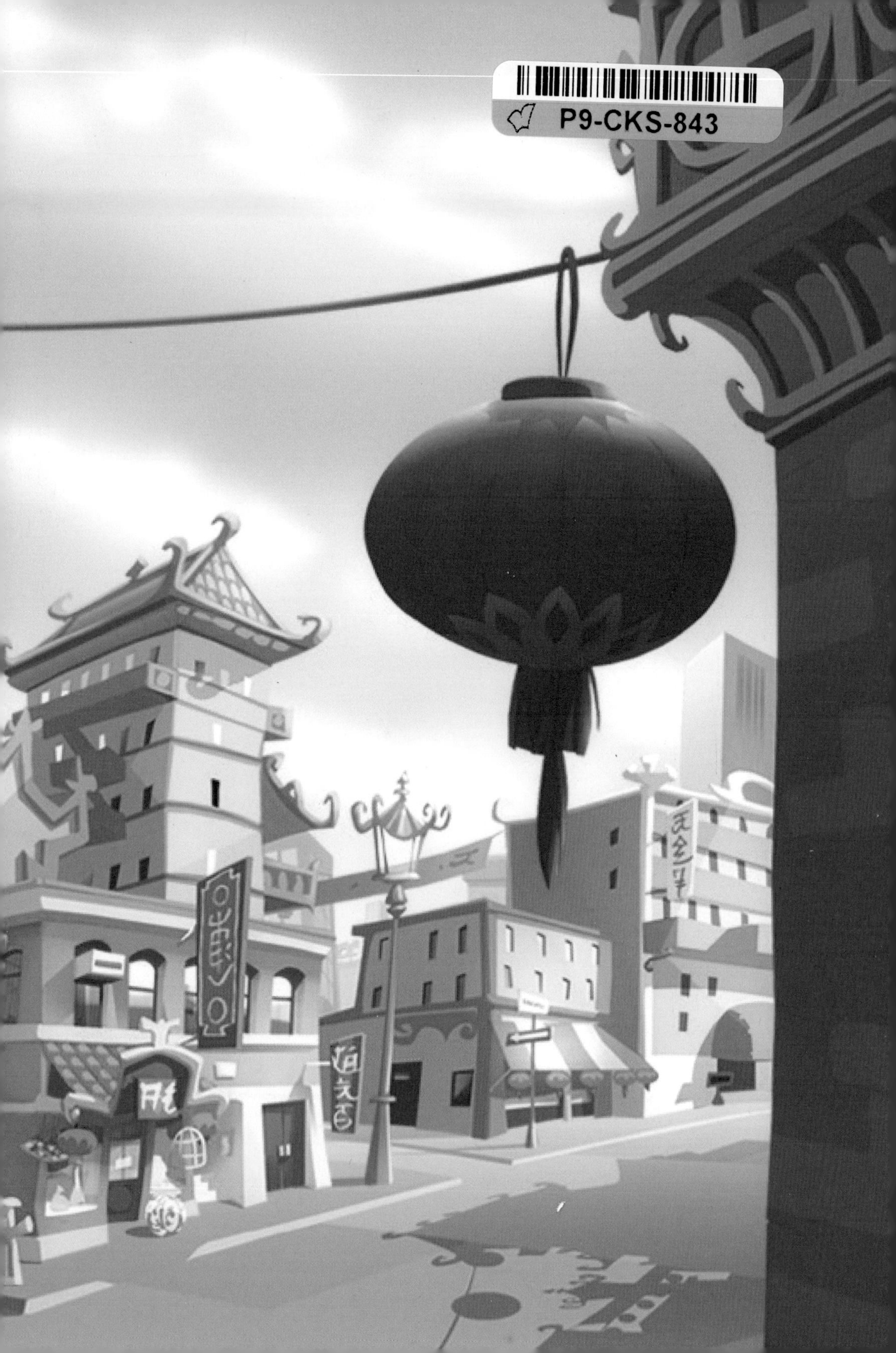

Geronimo Stilton™ Reporter

PAPERCUTZ™

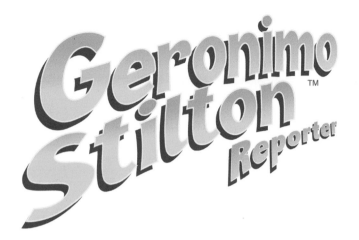

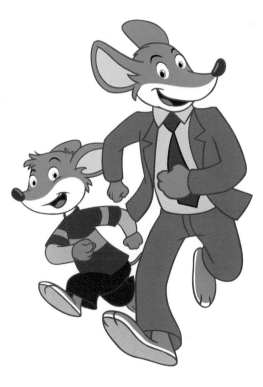

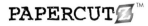

Geronimo Stilton

#1
"The Discovery
of America"

#2
"The Secret
of the Sphinx"

#3
"The Coliseum
Con"

#4
"Following the
Trail of Marco Polo"

#5
"The Great
Ice Age"

#6
"Who Stole
The Mona Lisa?"

#7
"Dinosaurs
in Action"

#8
"Play It Again,
Mozart!"

#9
"The Weird
Book Machine"

#10
"Geronimo Stilton
Saves the Olympics"

#11
"We'll Always
Have Paris"

#12
"The First Samurai"

#13
"The Fastest Train
in the West"

#14
"The First Mouse
on the Moon"

#15
"All for Stilton,
Stilton for All!"

#16
"Lights, Camera,
Stilton!"

#17
"The Mystery of the
Pirate Ship"

#18
"First to the Last Place
on Earth"

#19
"Lost in Translation"

GERONIMO
STILTON REPORTER #1
"Operation ShuFongFong"

GERONIMO
STILTON REPORTER #2
"It's My Scoop"

GERONIMO
STILTON REPORTER #3
"Stop Acting Around"

GERONIMO
STILTON REPORTER #4
"The Mummy with No Name"

GERONIMO
STILTON REPORTER #5
"Barry the Moustache"

COMING SOON

GERONIMO
STILTON REPORTER #6
"Paws Off, Cheddarface!"

GERONIMO
STILTON REPORTER #8
"Hypno-Tick Tock"

GERONIMO STILTON
3 in 1 #1

GERONIMO STILTON
3 in 1 #2

GERONIMO STILTON
3 in 1 #3

**...ALSO
AVAILABLE
WHEREVER
E-BOOKS
ARE SOLD!**

See more at papercutz.com

WITHDRAWN

#7 GOING DOWN TO CHINATOWN
By Geronimo Stilton

PAPERCUTZ™

NEW YORK

GOING DOWN TO CHINATOWN

Text by Geronimo Stilton
Cover by ALESSANDRO MUSCILLO (artist) and CHRISTIAN ALIPRANDI (colorist)
Editorial supervision by ALESSANDRA BERELLO (Atlantyca S.p.A.)
Editing by ANITA DENTI (Atlantyca S.p.A.)
Script by DARIO SICCHIO
Art by ALESSANDRO MUSCILLO
Color by CHRISTIAN ALIPRANDI
Original Lettering by MARIA LETIZIA MIRABELLA

Special thanks to CARMEN CASTILLO

TM & © Atlantyca S.p.A. Animated Series © 2010 Atlantyca S.p.A.– All Rights Reserved
International Rights © Atlantyca S.p.A., via Leopardi 8 - 20123 Milano - Italia - foreignrights@atlantyca.it - www.atlantyca.com
© 2021 for this Work in English language by Papercutz, 160 Broadway, Suite 700, East Wing, New York, NY 10038
www.papercutz.com

Based on an original idea by ELISABETTA DAMI.
Based on episode 7 of the Geronimo Stilton animated series "*Rotta verso la Cina*" ["Going Down to Chinatown"] written by LAURIE
ISRAEL & RACHEL RUDERMAN, storyboard by NICHOLAS MOSHINI
Preview based on episode 8 of the Geronimo Stilton animated series "*A me gil occhi*" ["Hypno-Tick Tock"] written by CHARLOTTE
FULLERTON, storyboard by PIER DI GIÀ & PATRIZIA NASI

www.geronimostilton.com

JAYJAY JACKSON — Production
WILSON RAMOS JR. — Lettering
JEFF WHITMAN — Managing Editor
INGRID RIOS — Editorial Intern
JIM SALICRUP
Editor-in-Chief

ISBN: 978-1-5458-0617-3

Printed in China
March 2021

Papercutz books may be purchased for business or promotional use.
For information on bulk purchases please contact
Macmillan Corporate and Premium Sales
Department at (800) 221-7945x5442.

Distributed by Macmillan
First Printing

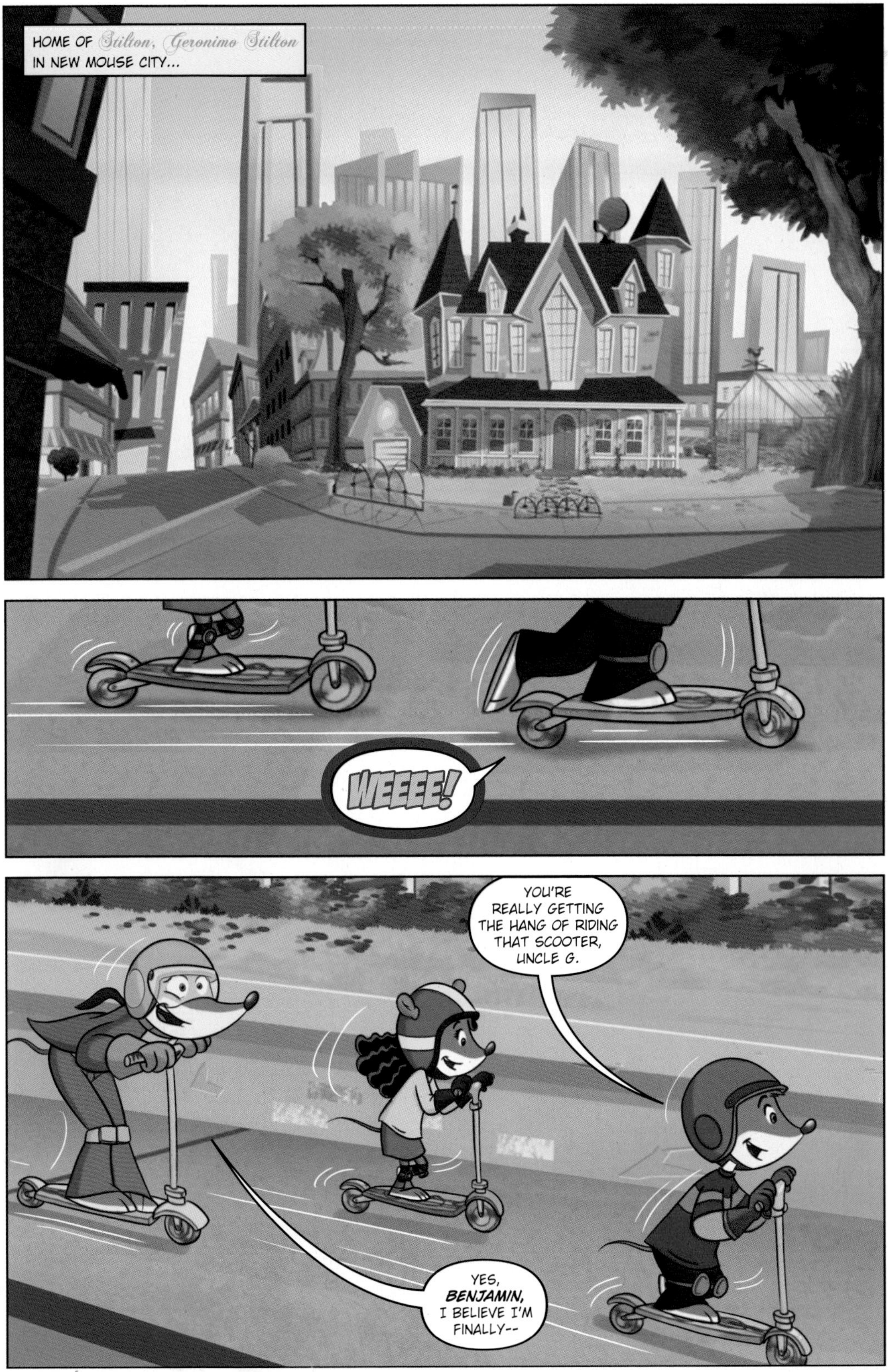
HOME OF Stilton, Geronimo Stilton
IN NEW MOUSE CITY...
WEEEE!
YOU'RE REALLY GETTING THE HANG OF RIDING THAT SCOOTER, UNCLE G.
YES, BENJAMIN, I BELIEVE I'M FINALLY--

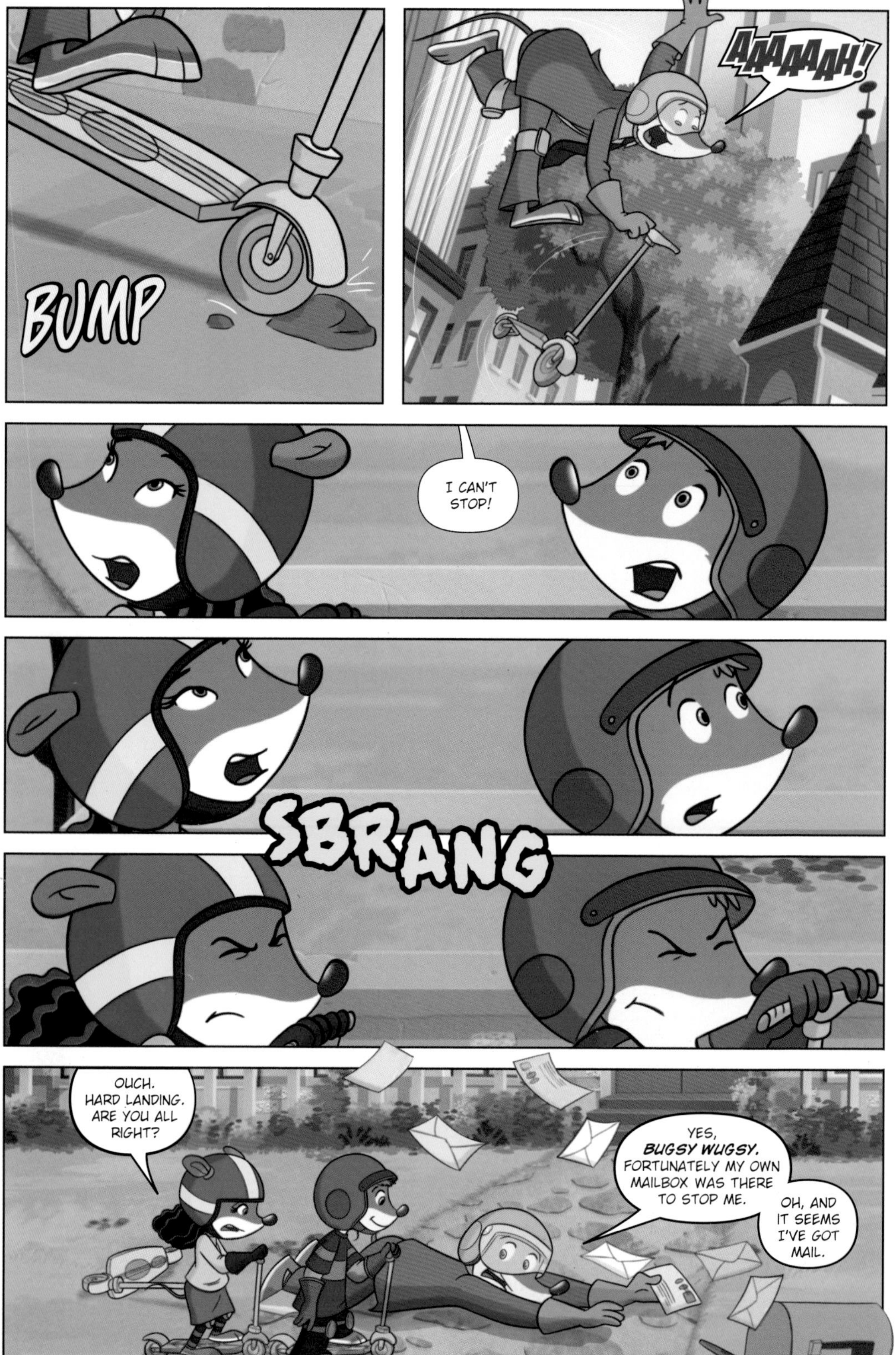
BUMP
AAAAAAH!
I CAN'T STOP!
SBRANG
OUCH. HARD LANDING. ARE YOU ALL RIGHT?
YES, ***BUGSY WUGSY.*** FORTUNATELY MY OWN MAILBOX WAS THERE TO STOP ME.
OH, AND IT SEEMS I'VE GOT MAIL.

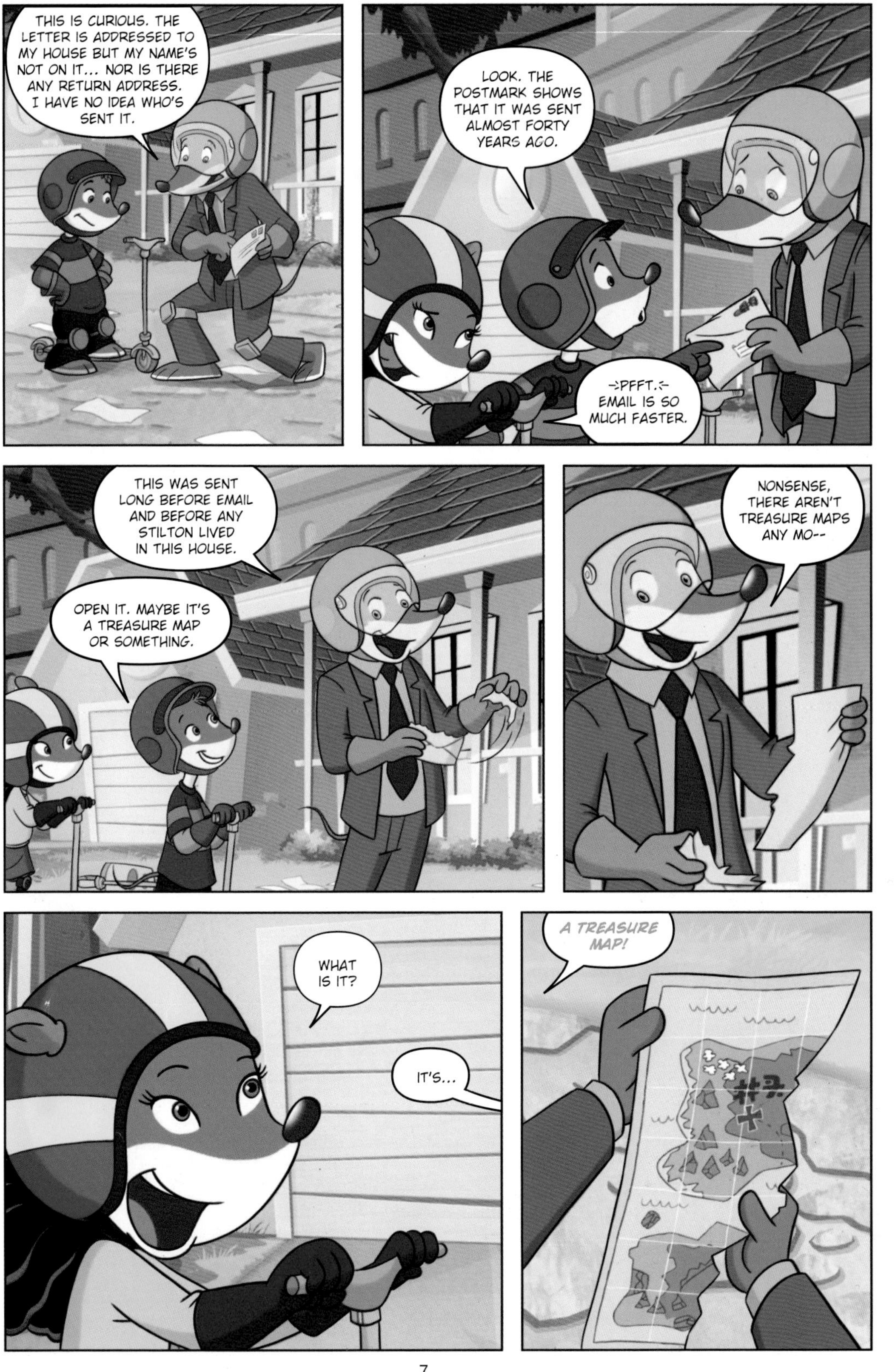
THIS IS CURIOUS. THE LETTER IS ADDRESSED TO MY HOUSE BUT MY NAME'S NOT ON IT... NOR IS THERE ANY RETURN ADDRESS. I HAVE NO IDEA WHO'S SENT IT.
LOOK. THE POSTMARK SHOWS THAT IT WAS SENT ALMOST FORTY YEARS AGO.
PFFT. EMAIL IS SO MUCH FASTER.
THIS WAS SENT LONG BEFORE EMAIL AND BEFORE ANY STILTON LIVED IN THIS HOUSE.
OPEN IT. MAYBE IT'S A TREASURE MAP OR SOMETHING.
NONSENSE, THERE AREN'T TREASURE MAPS ANY MO--
WHAT IS IT?
IT'S...
A TREASURE MAP!

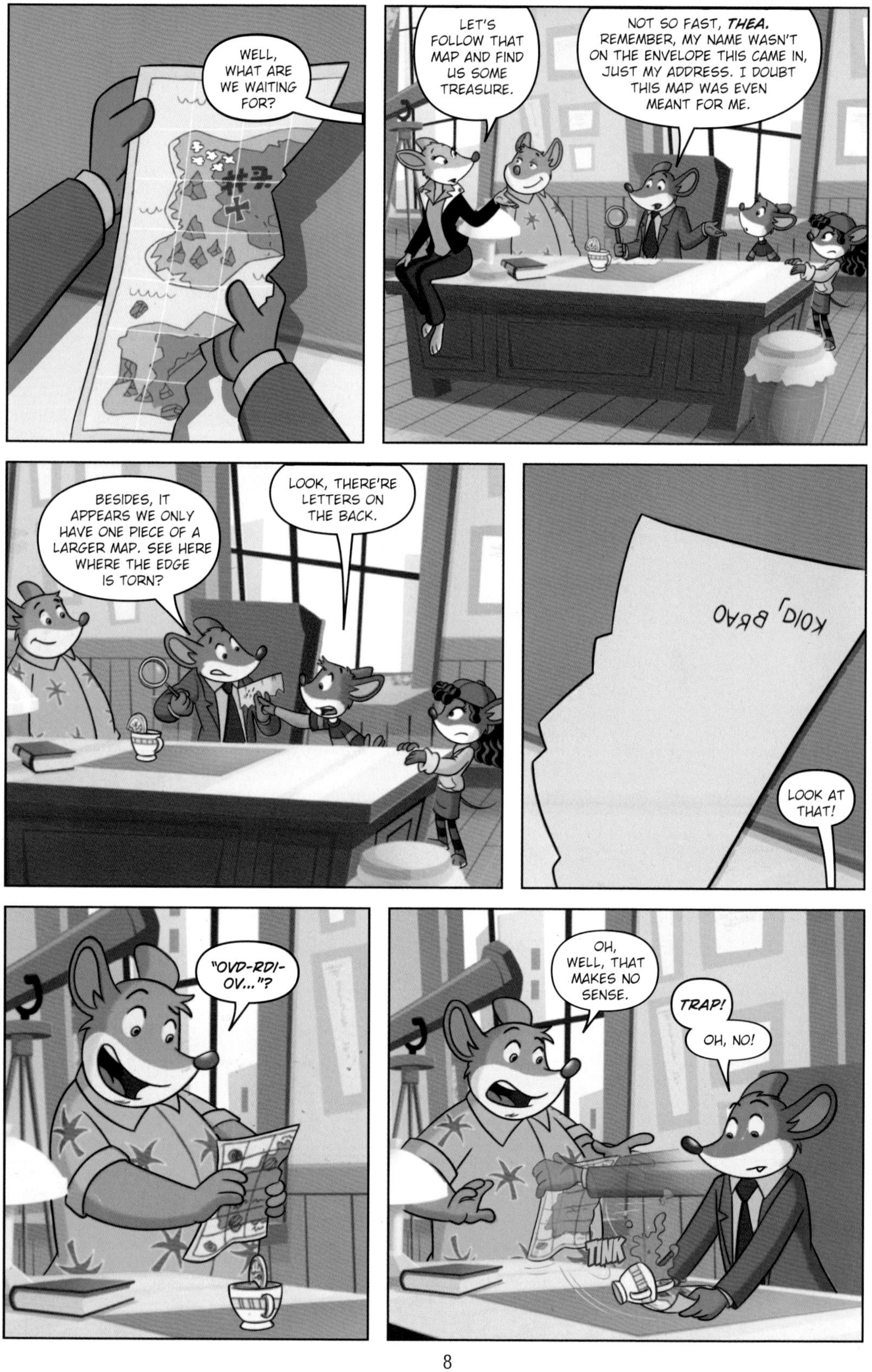
WELL, WHAT ARE WE WAITING FOR?
LET'S FOLLOW THAT MAP AND FIND US SOME TREASURE.
NOT SO FAST, ***THEA.*** REMEMBER, MY NAME WASN'T ON THE ENVELOPE THIS CAME IN, JUST MY ADDRESS. I DOUBT THIS MAP WAS EVEN MEANT FOR ME.
BESIDES, IT APPEARS WE ONLY HAVE ONE PIECE OF A LARGER MAP. SEE HERE WHERE THE EDGE IS TORN?
LOOK, THERE'RE LETTERS ON THE BACK.
LOOK AT THAT!
"OVD-RDI-OV..."?
OH, WELL, THAT MAKES NO SENSE.
TRAP!
OH, NO!
TINK

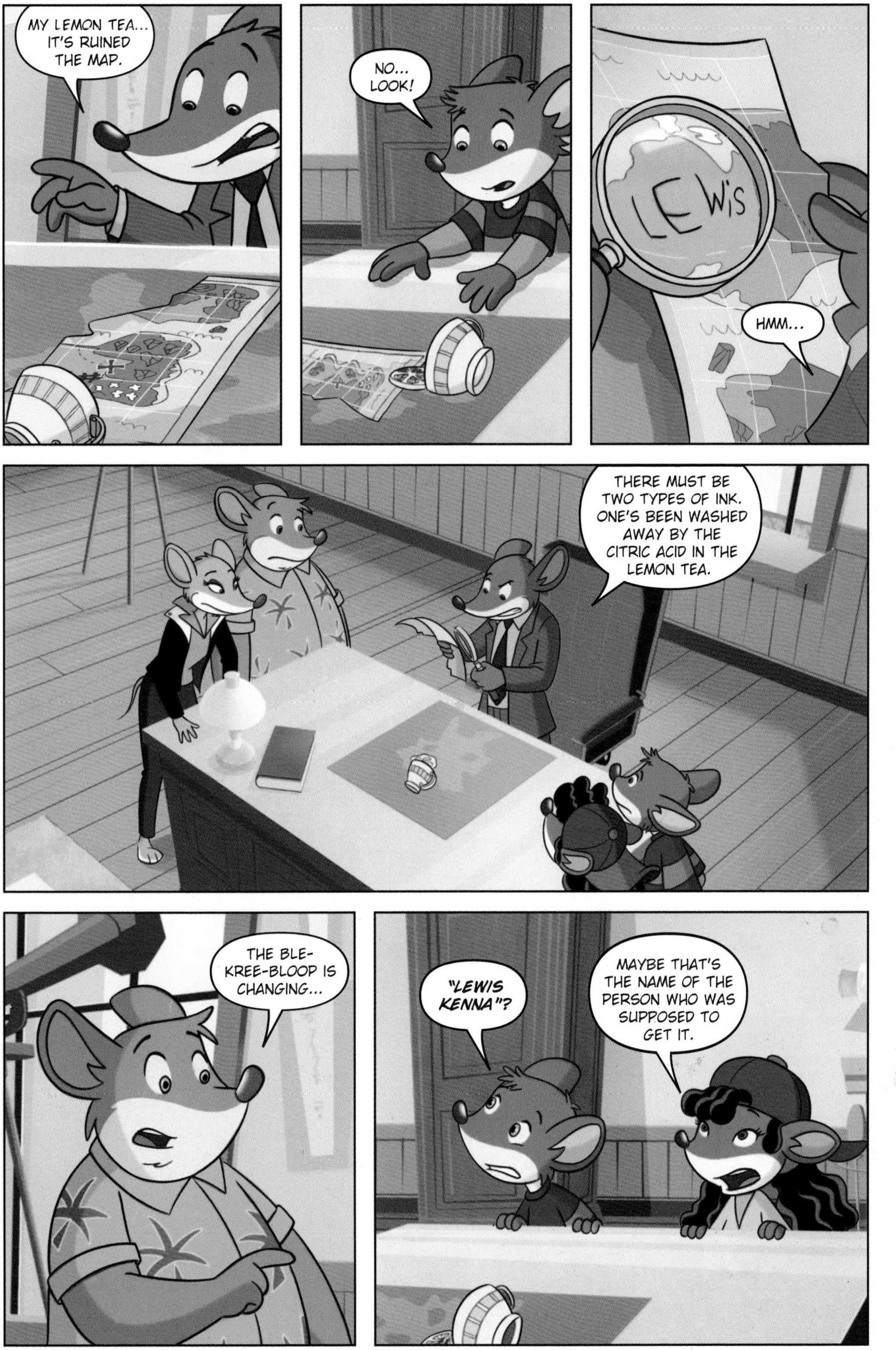
MY LEMON TEA... IT'S RUINED THE MAP.
NO... LOOK!
LEWIS
HMM...
THERE MUST BE TWO TYPES OF INK. ONE'S BEEN WASHED AWAY BY THE CITRIC ACID IN THE LEMON TEA.
THE BLE-KREE-BLOOP IS CHANGING...
"LEWIS KENNA"?
MAYBE THAT'S THE NAME OF THE PERSON WHO WAS SUPPOSED TO GET IT.

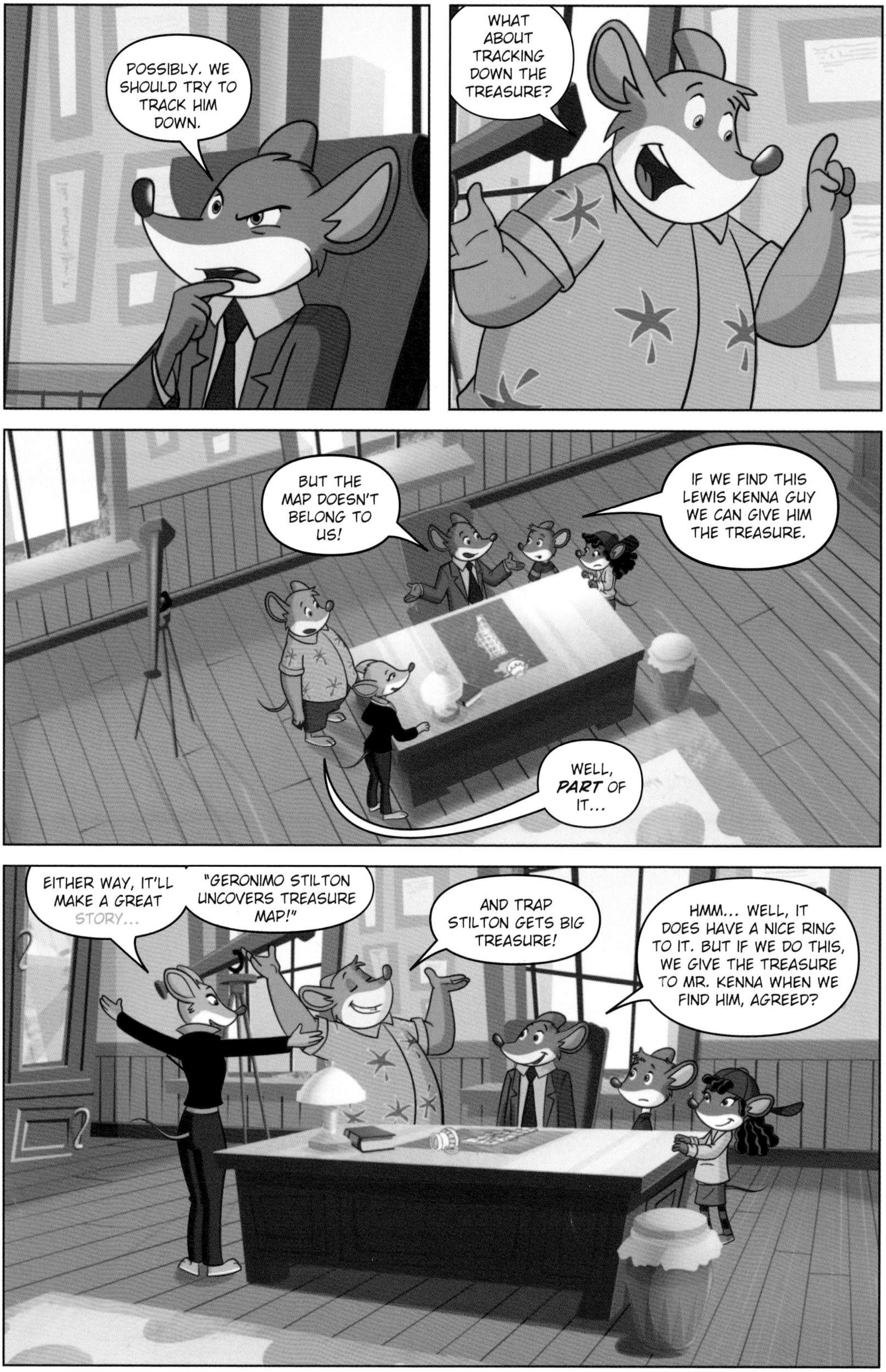
POSSIBLY. WE SHOULD TRY TO TRACK HIM DOWN.
WHAT ABOUT TRACKING DOWN THE TREASURE?
BUT THE MAP DOESN'T BELONG TO US!
IF WE FIND THIS LEWIS KENNA GUY WE CAN GIVE HIM THE TREASURE.
WELL, **PART** OF IT...
EITHER WAY, IT'LL MAKE A GREAT STORY...
"GERONIMO STILTON UNCOVERS TREASURE MAP!"
AND TRAP STILTON GETS BIG TREASURE!
HMM... WELL, IT DOES HAVE A NICE RING TO IT. BUT IF WE DO THIS, WE GIVE THE TREASURE TO MR. KENNA WHEN WE FIND HIM, AGREED?

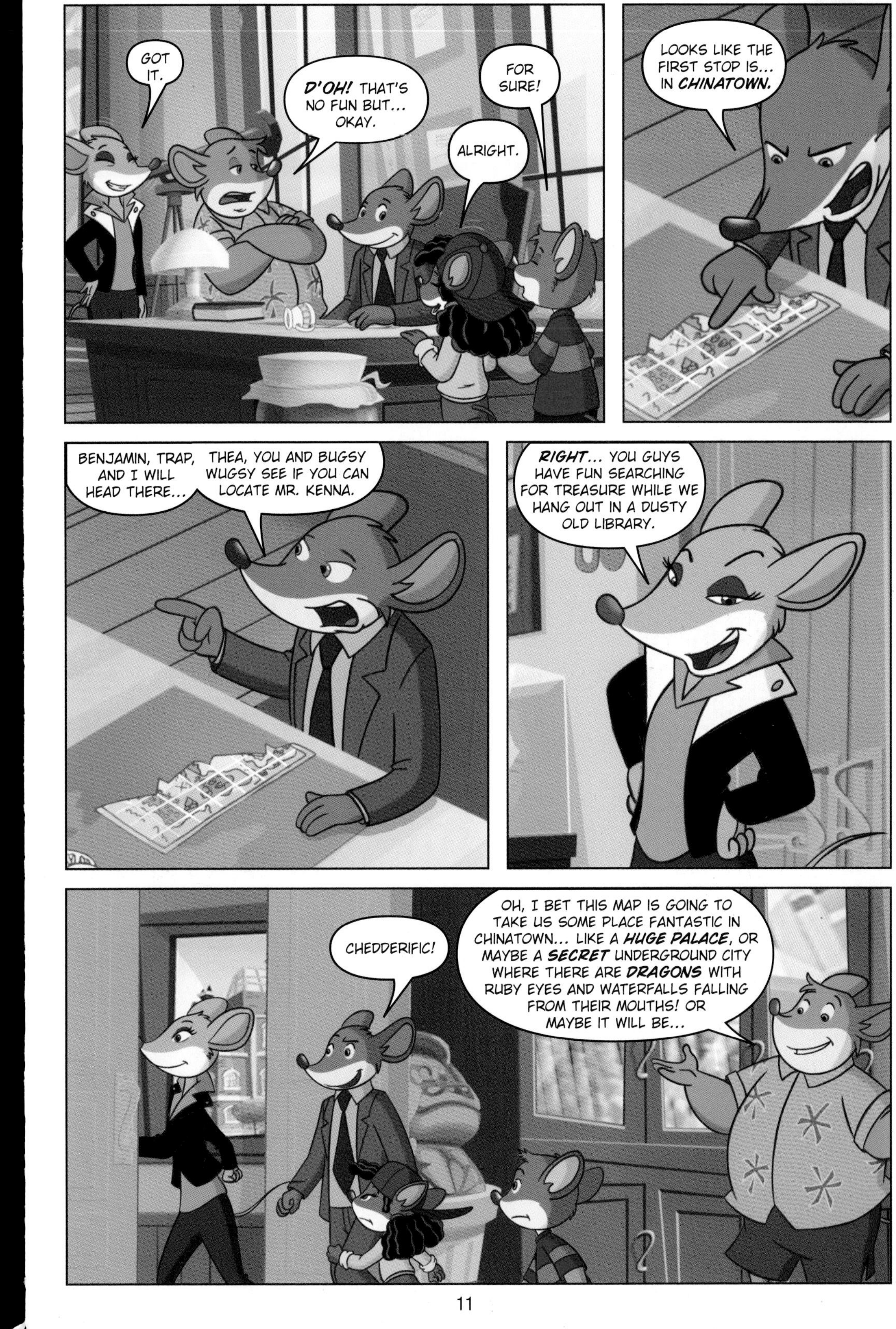
GOT IT.
D'OH! THAT'S NO FUN BUT... OKAY.
ALRIGHT.
FOR SURE!
LOOKS LIKE THE FIRST STOP IS... IN CHINATOWN.
BENJAMIN, TRAP, AND I WILL HEAD THERE...
THEA, YOU AND BUGSY WUGSY SEE IF YOU CAN LOCATE MR. KENNA.
RIGHT... YOU GUYS HAVE FUN SEARCHING FOR TREASURE WHILE WE HANG OUT IN A DUSTY OLD LIBRARY.
CHEDDERIFIC!
OH, I BET THIS MAP IS GOING TO TAKE US SOME PLACE FANTASTIC IN CHINATOWN... LIKE A HUGE PALACE, OR MAYBE A SECRET UNDERGROUND CITY WHERE THERE ARE DRAGONS WITH RUBY EYES AND WATERFALLS FALLING FROM THEIR MOUTHS! OR MAYBE IT WILL BE...

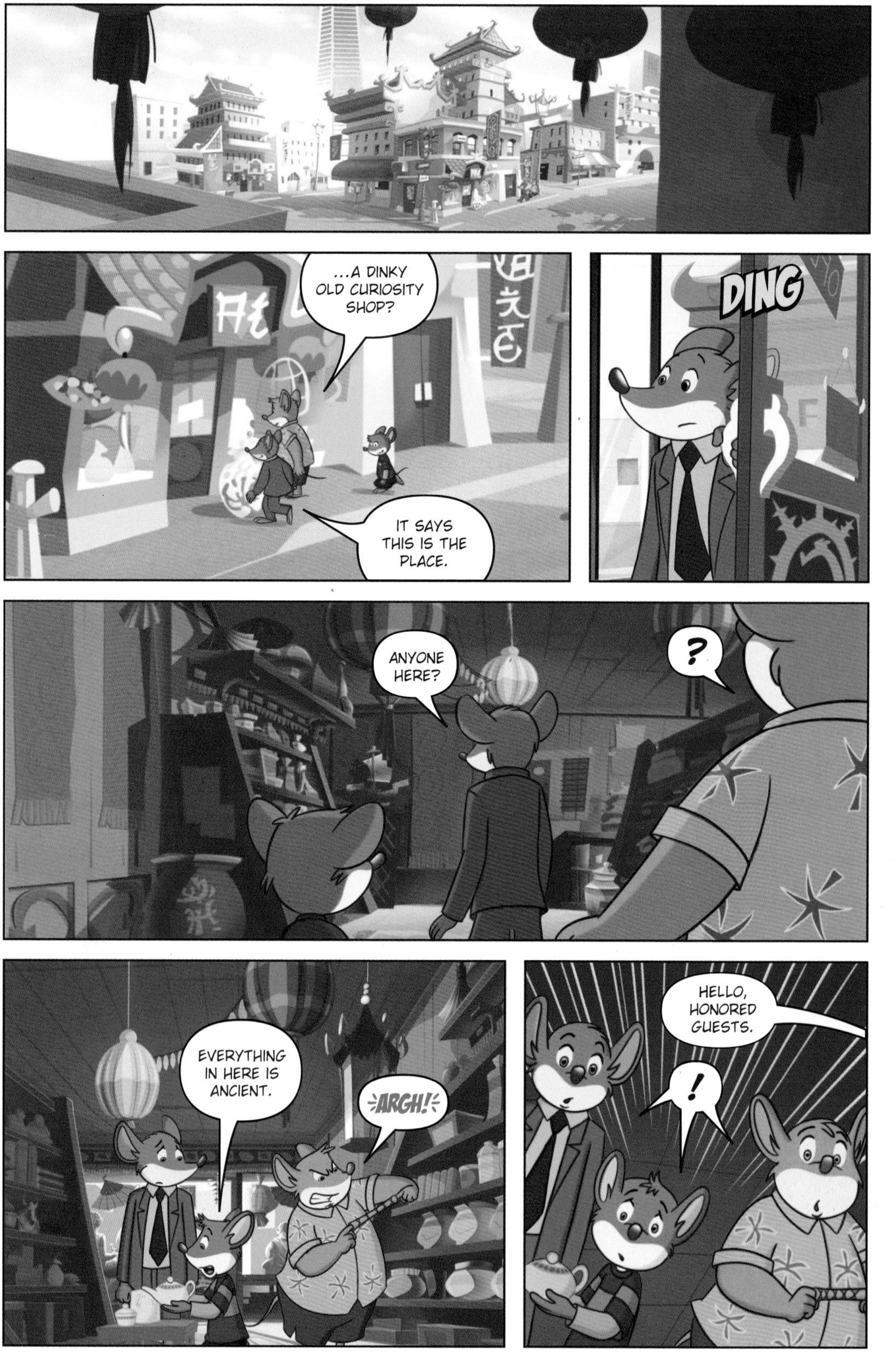
...A DINKY OLD CURIOSITY SHOP?
IT SAYS THIS IS THE PLACE.
DING
ANYONE HERE?
?
EVERYTHING IN HERE IS ANCIENT.
ARGH!
HELLO, HONORED GUESTS.
!

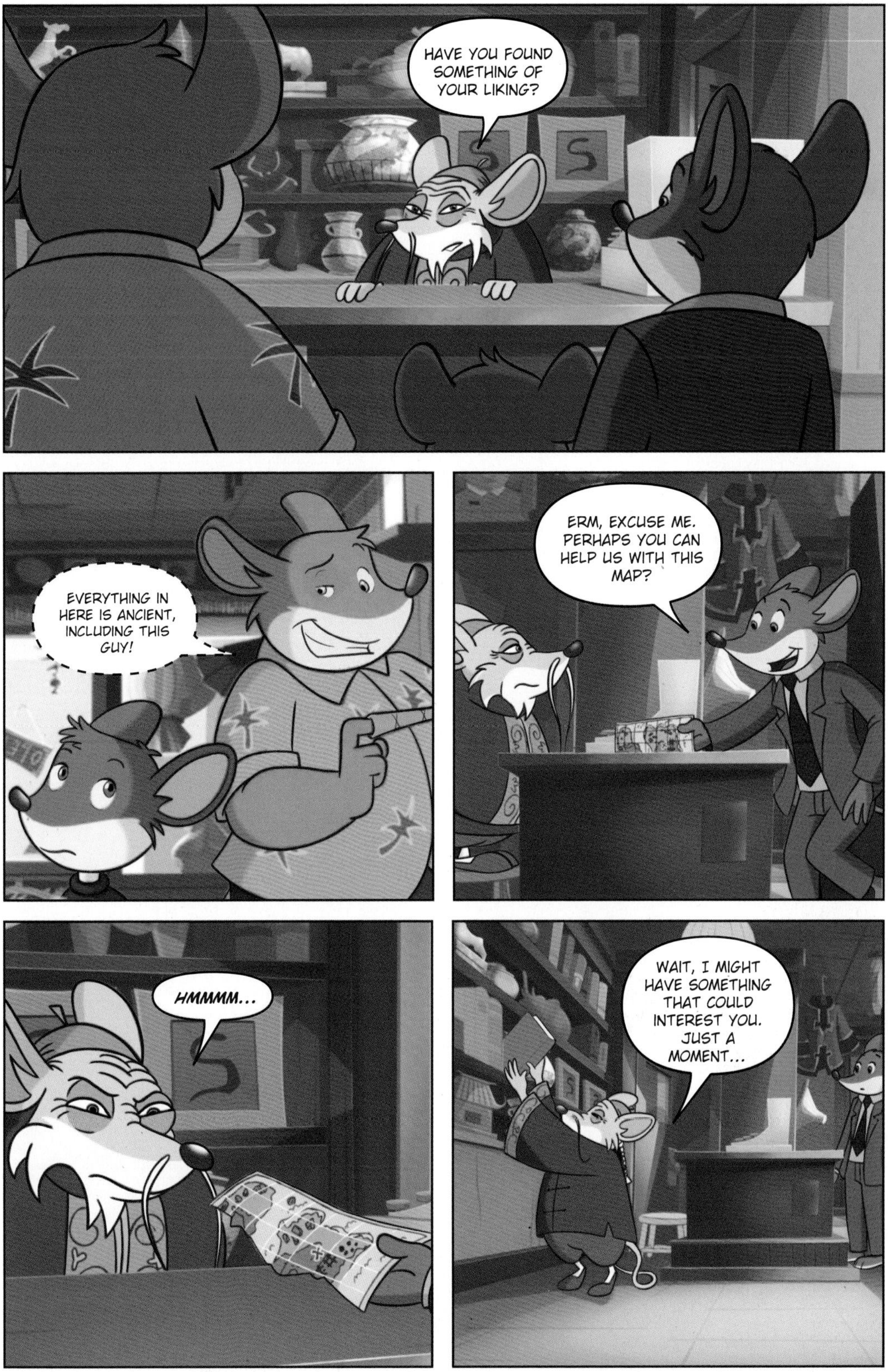
HAVE YOU FOUND SOMETHING OF YOUR LIKING?
EVERYTHING IN HERE IS ANCIENT, INCLUDING THIS GUY!
ERM, EXCUSE ME. PERHAPS YOU CAN HELP US WITH THIS MAP?
HMMMM...
WAIT, I MIGHT HAVE SOMETHING THAT COULD INTEREST YOU. JUST A MOMENT...

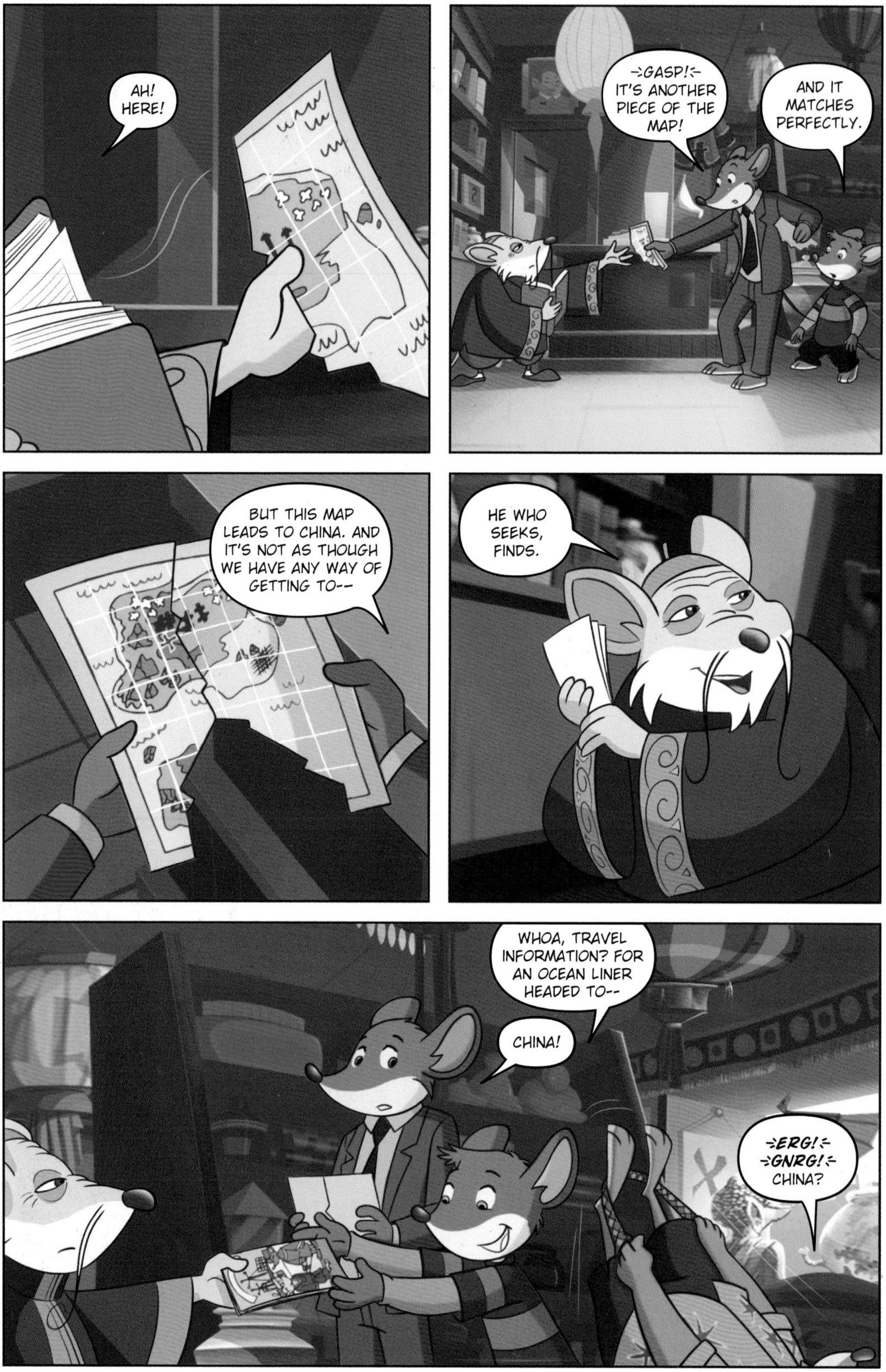
AH! HERE!
GASP! IT'S ANOTHER PIECE OF THE MAP!
AND IT MATCHES PERFECTLY.
BUT THIS MAP LEADS TO CHINA. AND IT'S NOT AS THOUGH WE HAVE ANY WAY OF GETTING TO--
HE WHO SEEKS, FINDS.
WHOA, TRAVEL INFORMATION? FOR AN OCEAN LINER HEADED TO--
CHINA!
ERG! GNRG! CHINA?

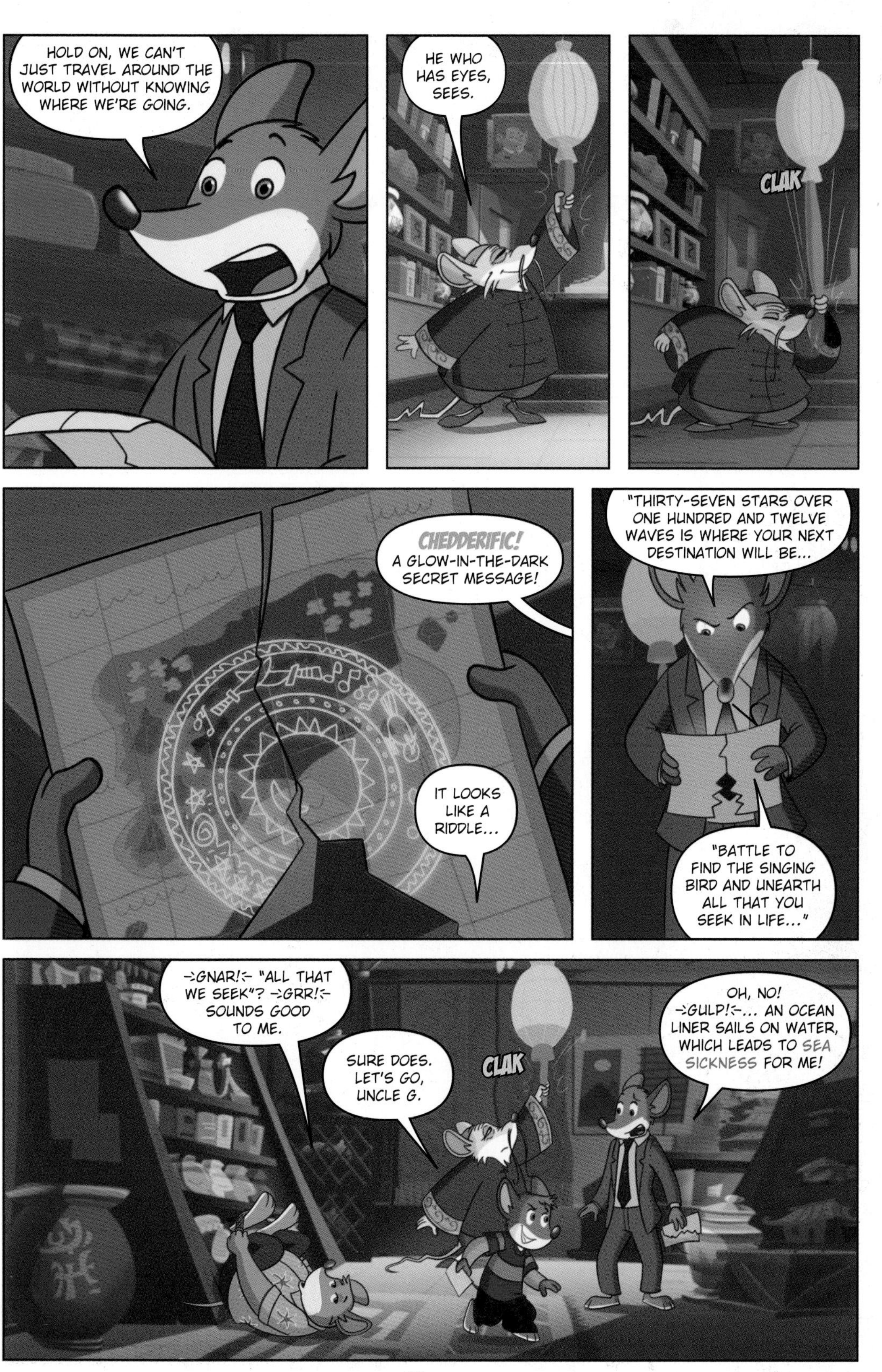
HOLD ON, WE CAN'T JUST TRAVEL AROUND THE WORLD WITHOUT KNOWING WHERE WE'RE GOING.
HE WHO HAS EYES, SEES.
CLAK
CHEDDERIFIC! A GLOW-IN-THE-DARK SECRET MESSAGE!
IT LOOKS LIKE A RIDDLE...
"THIRTY-SEVEN STARS OVER ONE HUNDRED AND TWELVE WAVES IS WHERE YOUR NEXT DESTINATION WILL BE...
"BATTLE TO FIND THE SINGING BIRD AND UNEARTH ALL THAT YOU SEEK IN LIFE..."
-GNAR!- "ALL THAT WE SEEK"? -GRR!- SOUNDS GOOD TO ME.
SURE DOES. LET'S GO, UNCLE G.
CLAK
OH, NO! -GULP!-... AN OCEAN LINER SAILS ON WATER, WHICH LEADS TO SEA SICKNESS FOR ME!

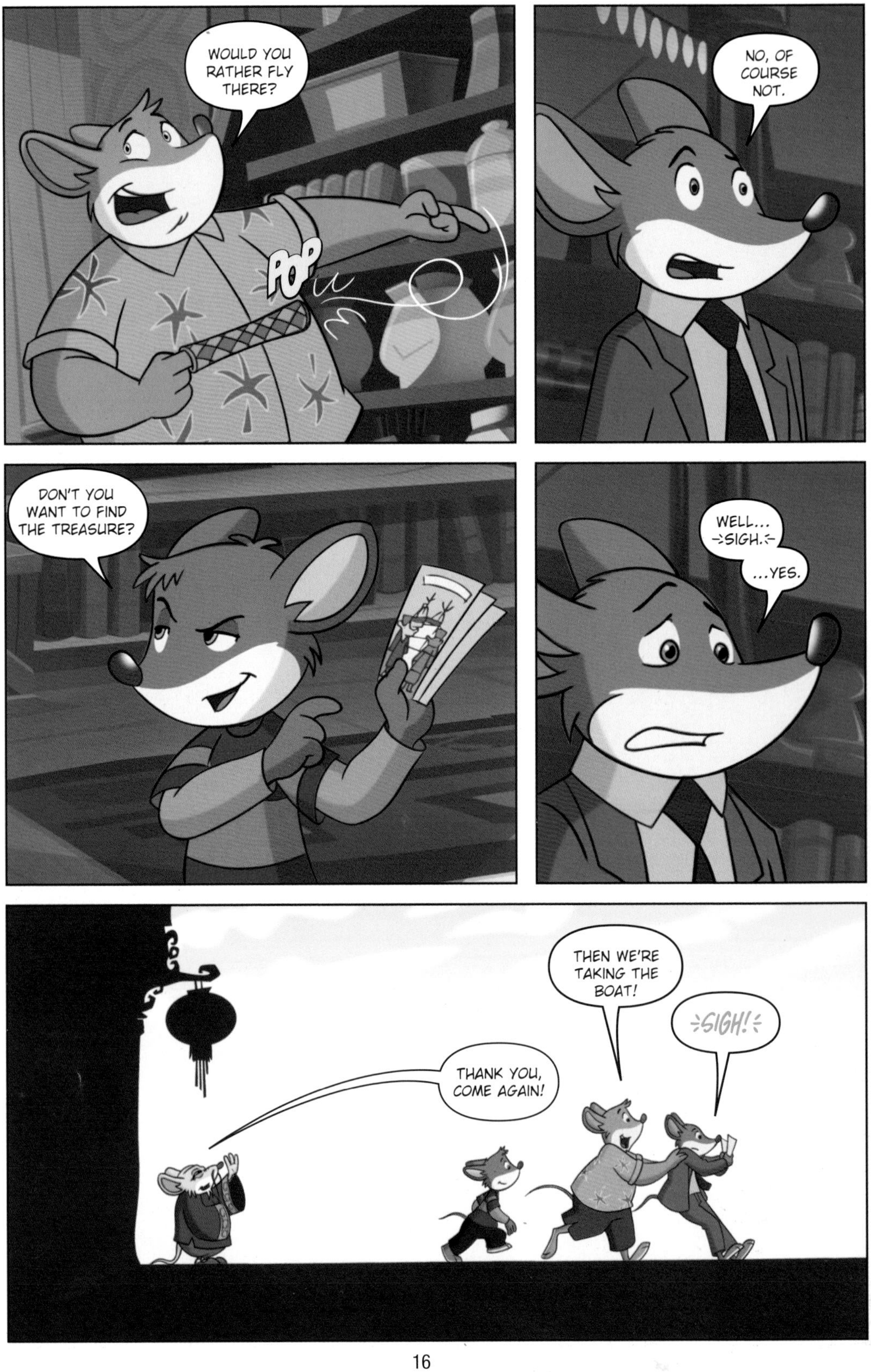
WOULD YOU RATHER FLY THERE?
POP
NO, OF COURSE NOT.
DON'T YOU WANT TO FIND THE TREASURE?
WELL... -SIGH.-
...YES.
THANK YOU, COME AGAIN!
THEN WE'RE TAKING THE BOAT!
SIGH!

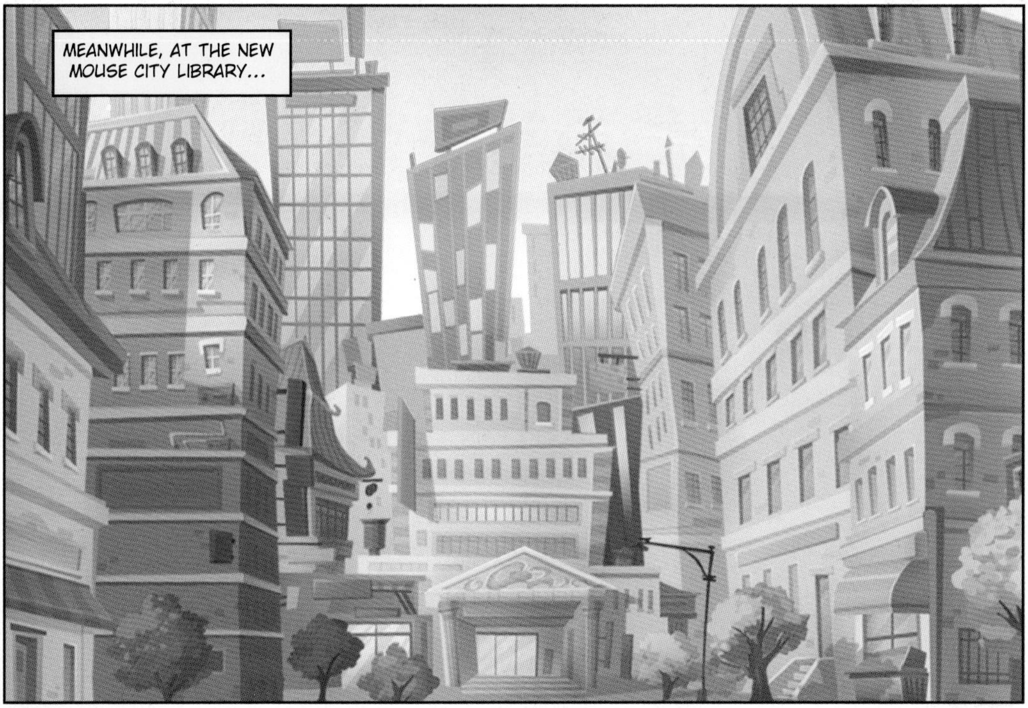
MEANWHILE, AT THE NEW MOUSE CITY LIBRARY...

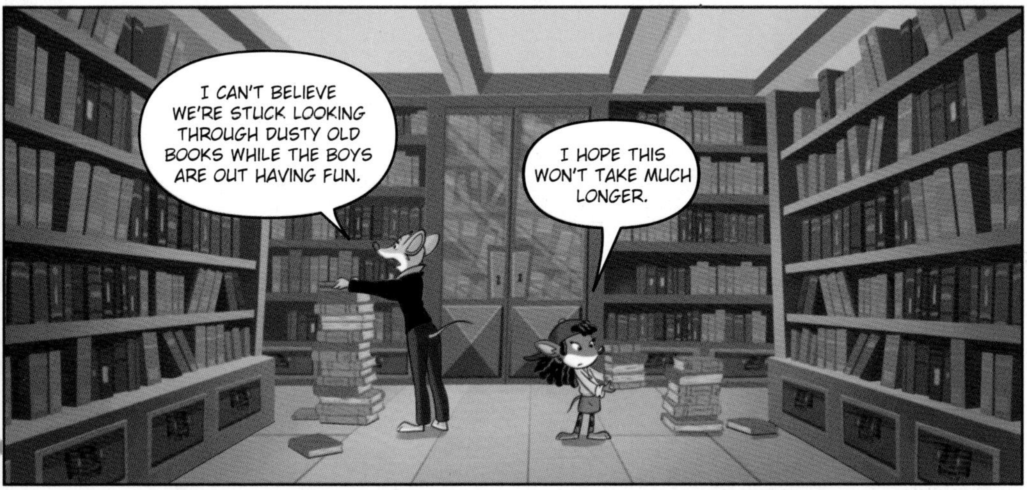
I CAN'T BELIEVE WE'RE STUCK LOOKING THROUGH DUSTY OLD BOOKS WHILE THE BOYS ARE OUT HAVING FUN.
I HOPE THIS WON'T TAKE MUCH LONGER.

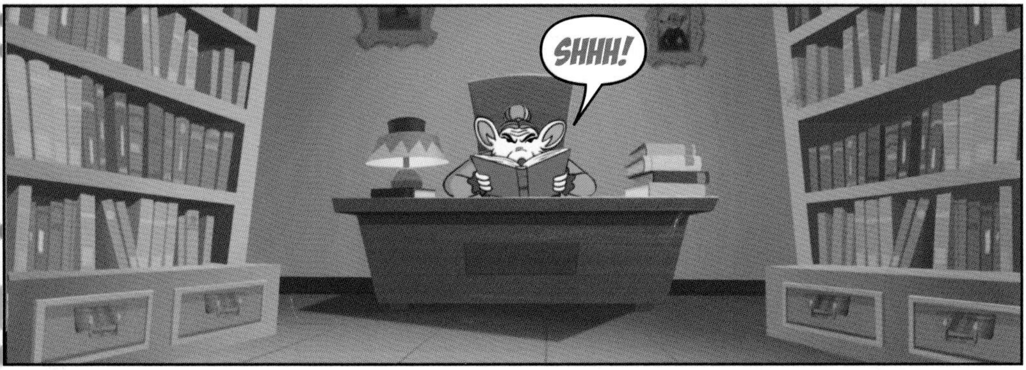
SHHH!

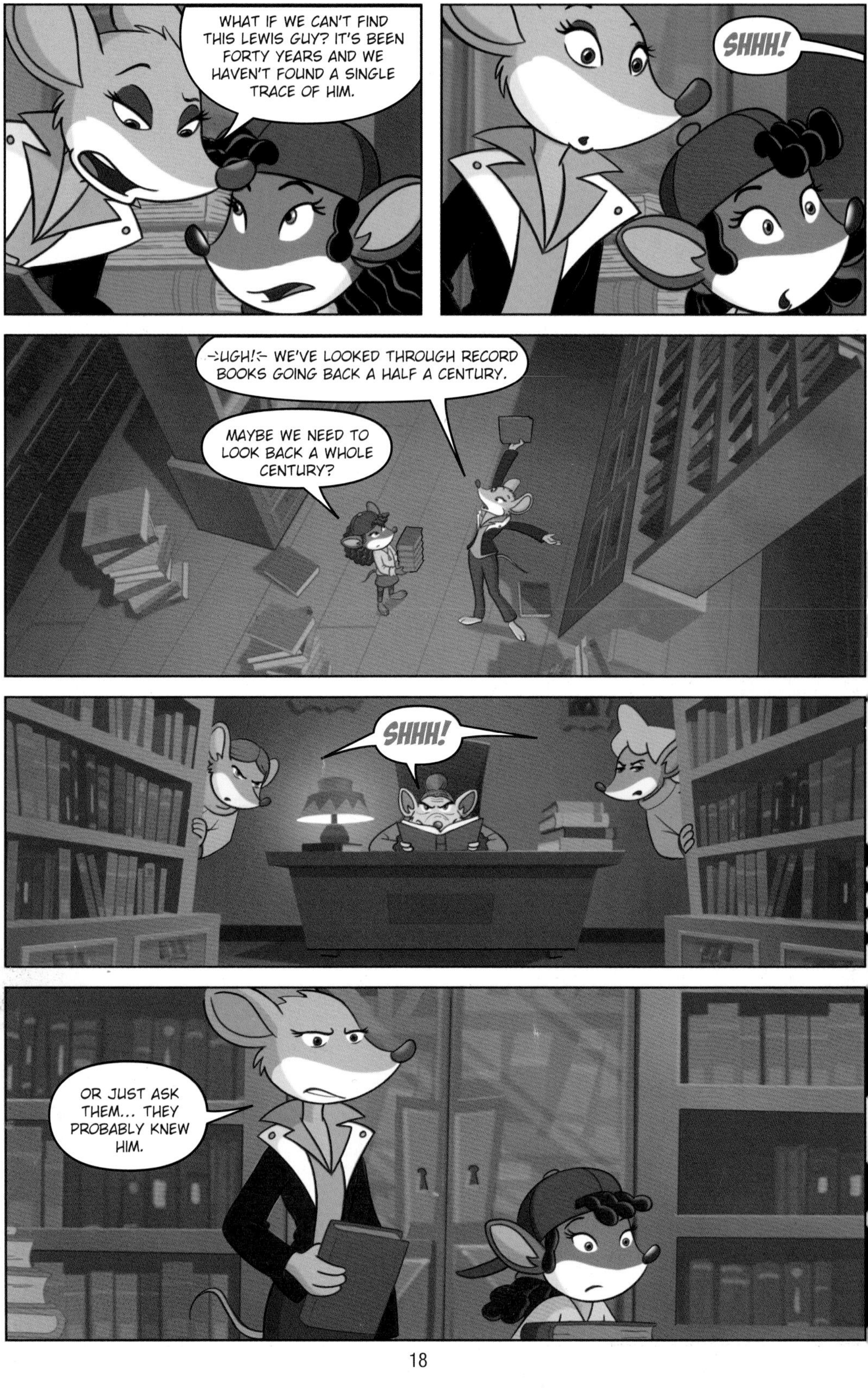

WHAT IF WE CAN'T FIND THIS LEWIS GUY? IT'S BEEN FORTY YEARS AND WE HAVEN'T FOUND A SINGLE TRACE OF HIM.
SHHH!
-UGH!- WE'VE LOOKED THROUGH RECORD BOOKS GOING BACK A HALF A CENTURY.
MAYBE WE NEED TO LOOK BACK A WHOLE CENTURY?
SHHH!
OR JUST ASK THEM... THEY PROBABLY KNEW HIM.

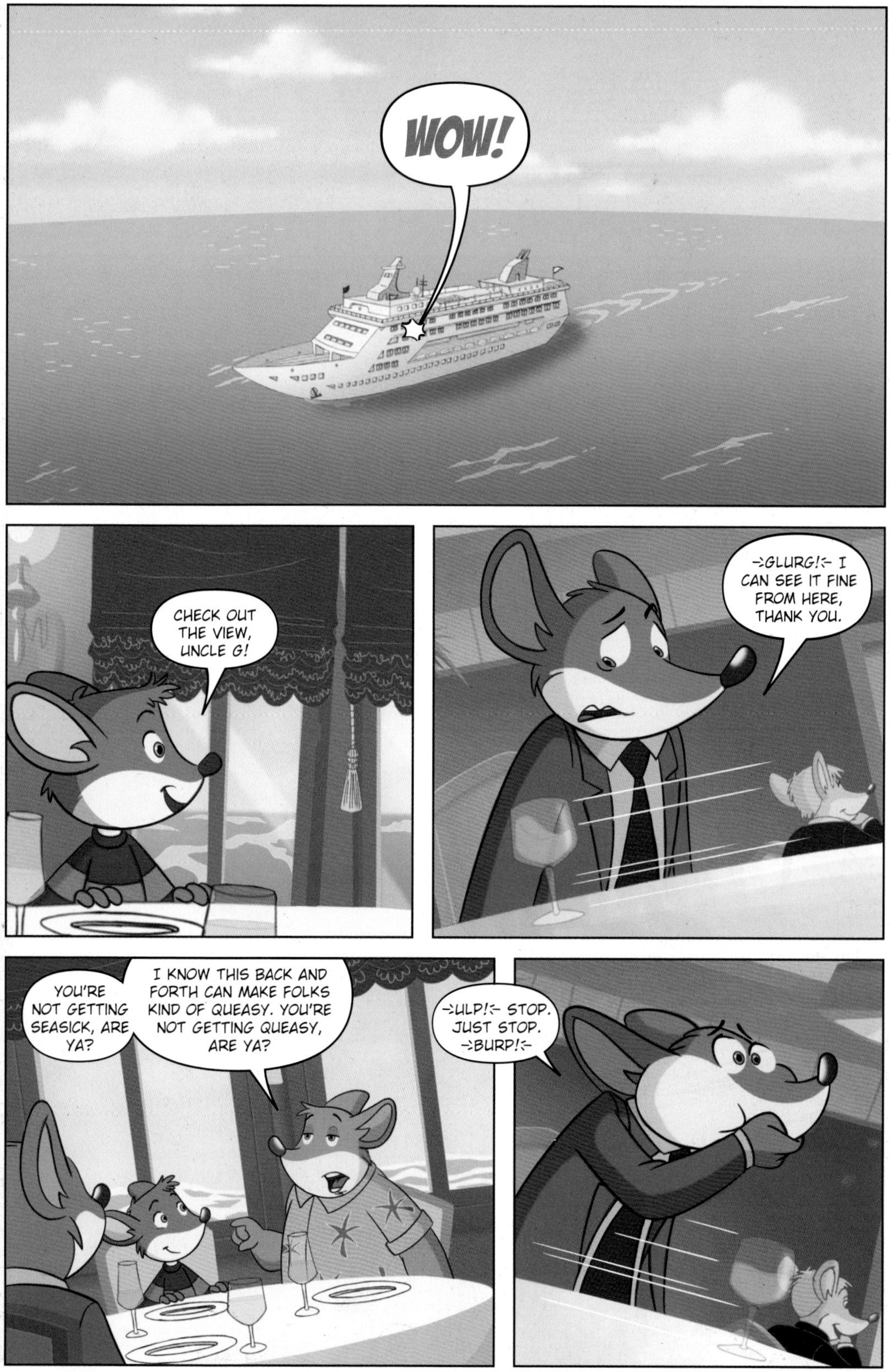
WOW!
CHECK OUT THE VIEW, UNCLE G!
-GLURG!- I CAN SEE IT FINE FROM HERE, THANK YOU.
YOU'RE NOT GETTING SEASICK, ARE YA?
I KNOW THIS BACK AND FORTH CAN MAKE FOLKS KIND OF QUEASY. YOU'RE NOT GETTING QUEASY, ARE YA?
-ULP!- STOP. JUST STOP. -BURP!-

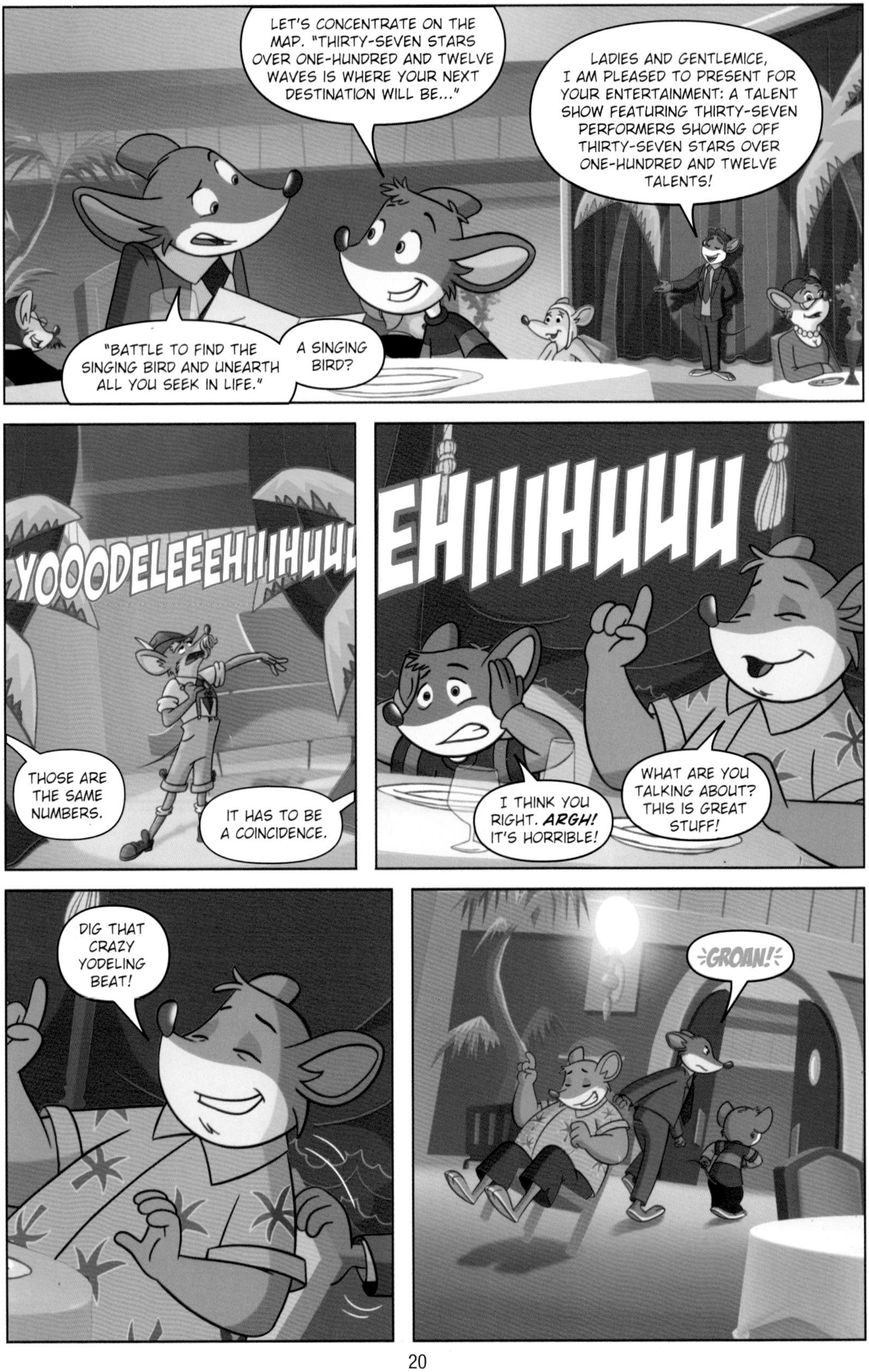

LET'S CONCENTRATE ON THE MAP. "THIRTY-SEVEN STARS OVER ONE-HUNDRED AND TWELVE WAVES IS WHERE YOUR NEXT DESTINATION WILL BE..."
"BATTLE TO FIND THE SINGING BIRD AND UNEARTH ALL YOU SEEK IN LIFE."
A SINGING BIRD?
LADIES AND GENTLEMICE, I AM PLEASED TO PRESENT FOR YOUR ENTERTAINMENT: A TALENT SHOW FEATURING THIRTY-SEVEN PERFORMERS SHOWING OFF THIRTY-SEVEN STARS OVER ONE-HUNDRED AND TWELVE TALENTS!
YOOODELEEEHIIIHUUU
EHIIIHUUU
THOSE ARE THE SAME NUMBERS.
IT HAS TO BE A COINCIDENCE.
I THINK YOU RIGHT. ARGH! IT'S HORRIBLE!
WHAT ARE YOU TALKING ABOUT? THIS IS GREAT STUFF!
DIG THAT CRAZY YODELING BEAT!
GROAN!

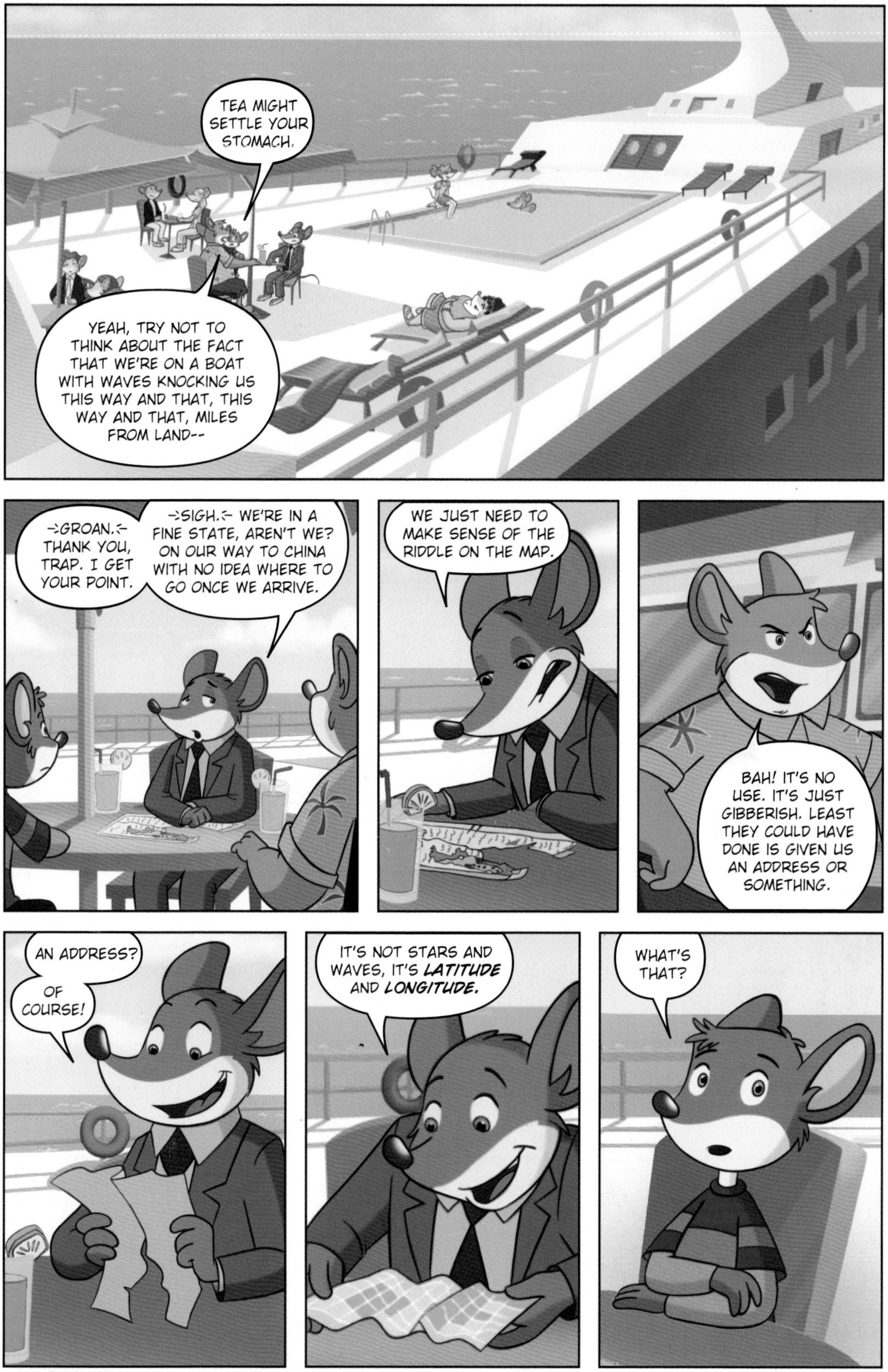
TEA MIGHT SETTLE YOUR STOMACH.
YEAH, TRY NOT TO THINK ABOUT THE FACT THAT WE'RE ON A BOAT WITH WAVES KNOCKING US THIS WAY AND THAT, THIS WAY AND THAT, MILES FROM LAND--
-GROAN.- THANK YOU, TRAP. I GET YOUR POINT.
-SIGH.- WE'RE IN A FINE STATE, AREN'T WE? ON OUR WAY TO CHINA WITH NO IDEA WHERE TO GO ONCE WE ARRIVE.
WE JUST NEED TO MAKE SENSE OF THE RIDDLE ON THE MAP.
BAH! IT'S NO USE. IT'S JUST GIBBERISH. LEAST THEY COULD HAVE DONE IS GIVEN US AN ADDRESS OR SOMETHING.
AN ADDRESS?
OF COURSE!
IT'S NOT STARS AND WAVES, IT'S ***LATITUDE*** AND ***LONGITUDE.***
WHAT'S THAT?

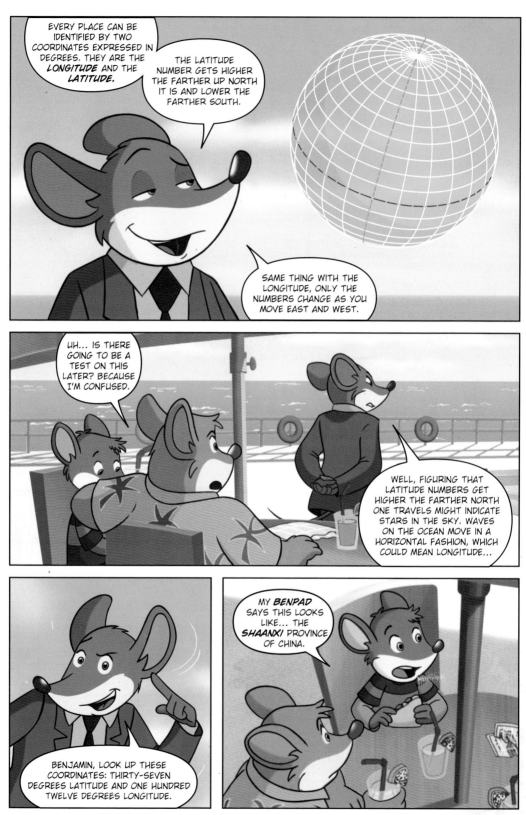

EVERY PLACE CAN BE IDENTIFIED BY TWO COORDINATES EXPRESSED IN DEGREES. THEY ARE THE *LONGITUDE* AND THE *LATITUDE.*

THE LATITUDE NUMBER GETS HIGHER THE FARTHER UP NORTH IT IS AND LOWER THE FARTHER SOUTH.

SAME THING WITH THE LONGITUDE, ONLY THE NUMBERS CHANGE AS YOU MOVE EAST AND WEST.

UH... IS THERE GOING TO BE A TEST ON THIS LATER? BECAUSE I'M CONFUSED.

WELL, FIGURING THAT LATITUDE NUMBERS GET HIGHER THE FARTHER NORTH ONE TRAVELS MIGHT INDICATE STARS IN THE SKY. WAVES ON THE OCEAN MOVE IN A HORIZONTAL FASHION, WHICH COULD MEAN LONGITUDE...

BENJAMIN, LOOK UP THESE COORDINATES: THIRTY-SEVEN DEGREES LATITUDE AND ONE HUNDRED TWELVE DEGREES LONGITUDE.

MY *BENPAD* SAYS THIS LOOKS LIKE... THE *SHAANXI* PROVINCE OF CHINA.

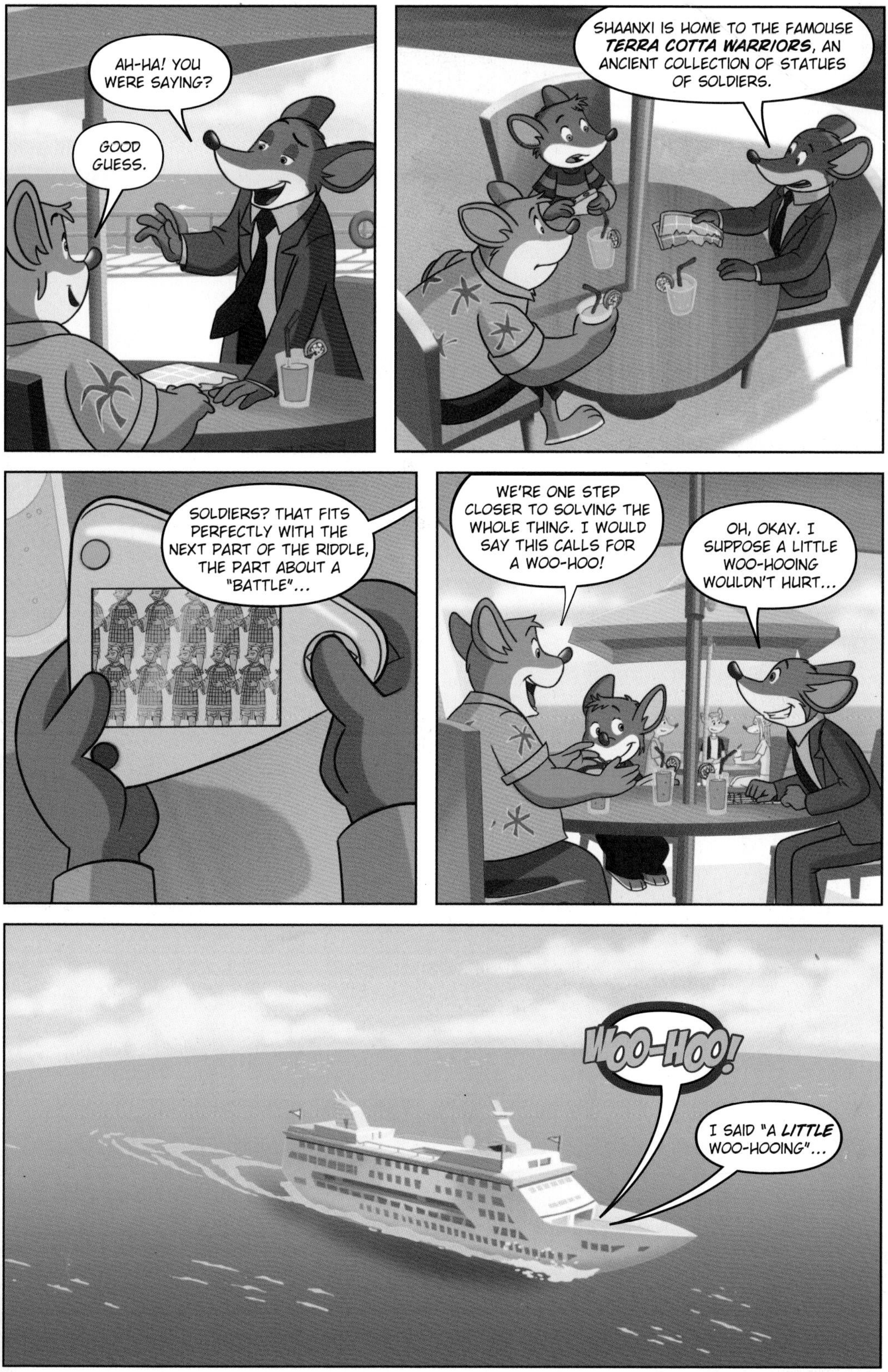
AH-HA! YOU WERE SAYING?
GOOD GUESS.
SHAANXI IS HOME TO THE FAMOUSE **TERRA COTTA WARRIORS**, AN ANCIENT COLLECTION OF STATUES OF SOLDIERS.
SOLDIERS? THAT FITS PERFECTLY WITH THE NEXT PART OF THE RIDDLE, THE PART ABOUT A "BATTLE"...
WE'RE ONE STEP CLOSER TO SOLVING THE WHOLE THING. I WOULD SAY THIS CALLS FOR A WOO-HOO!
OH, OKAY. I SUPPOSE A LITTLE WOO-HOOING WOULDN'T HURT...
WOO-HOO!
I SAID "A *LITTLE* WOO-HOOING"...

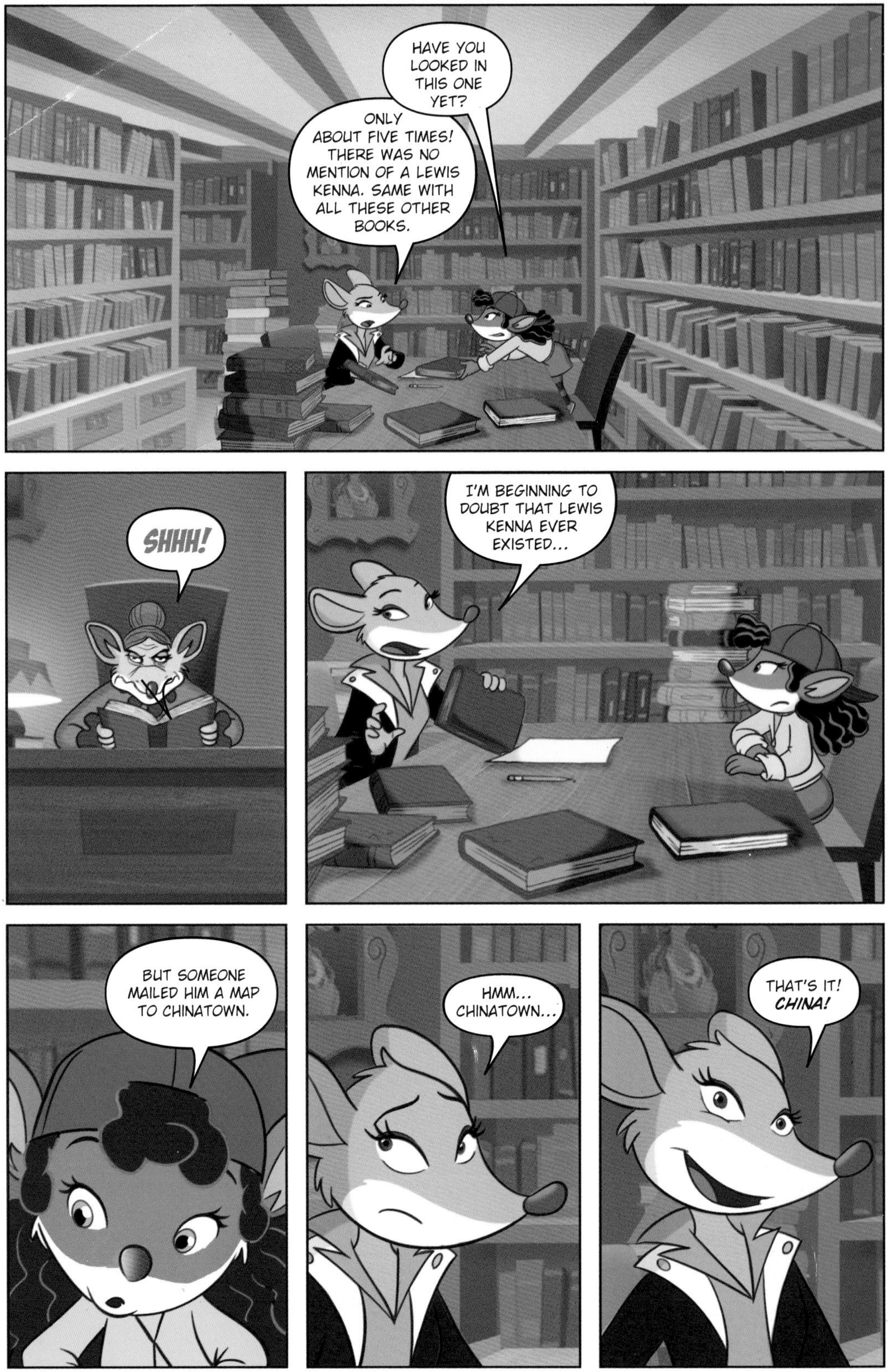
HAVE YOU LOOKED IN THIS ONE YET?
ONLY ABOUT FIVE TIMES! THERE WAS NO MENTION OF A LEWIS KENNA. SAME WITH ALL THESE OTHER BOOKS.
SHHH!
I'M BEGINNING TO DOUBT THAT LEWIS KENNA EVER EXISTED...
BUT SOMEONE MAILED HIM A MAP TO CHINATOWN.
HMM... CHINATOWN...
THAT'S IT! *CHINA!*

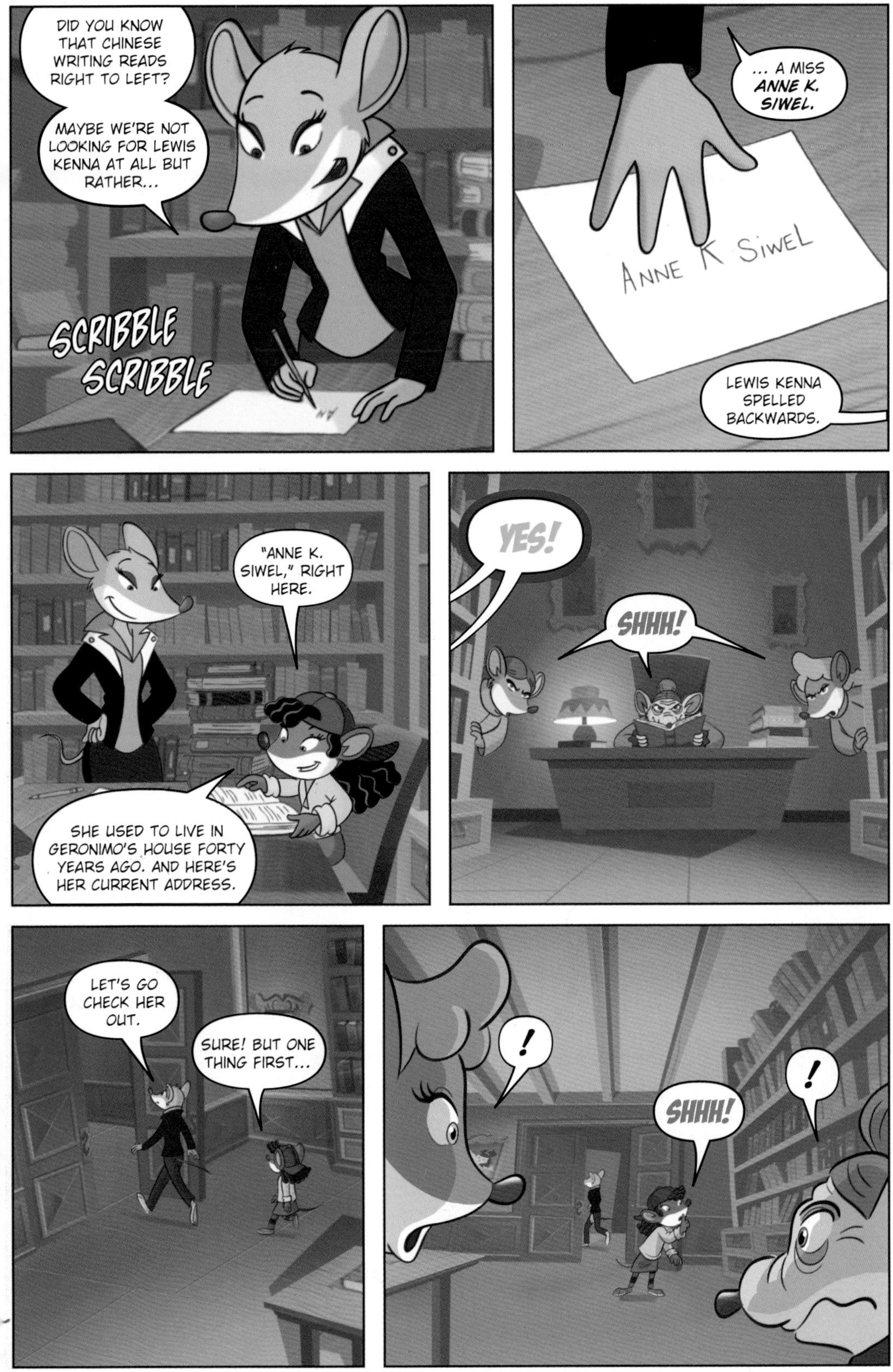
DID YOU KNOW THAT CHINESE WRITING READS RIGHT TO LEFT?
MAYBE WE'RE NOT LOOKING FOR LEWIS KENNA AT ALL BUT RATHER...
SCRIBBLE SCRIBBLE
... A MISS ANNE K. SIWEL.
ANNE K SIWEL
LEWIS KENNA SPELLED BACKWARDS.
"ANNE K. SIWEL," RIGHT HERE.
SHE USED TO LIVE IN GERONIMO'S HOUSE FORTY YEARS AGO. AND HERE'S HER CURRENT ADDRESS.
YES!
SHHH!
LET'S GO CHECK HER OUT.
SURE! BUT ONE THING FIRST...
!
SHHH!
!

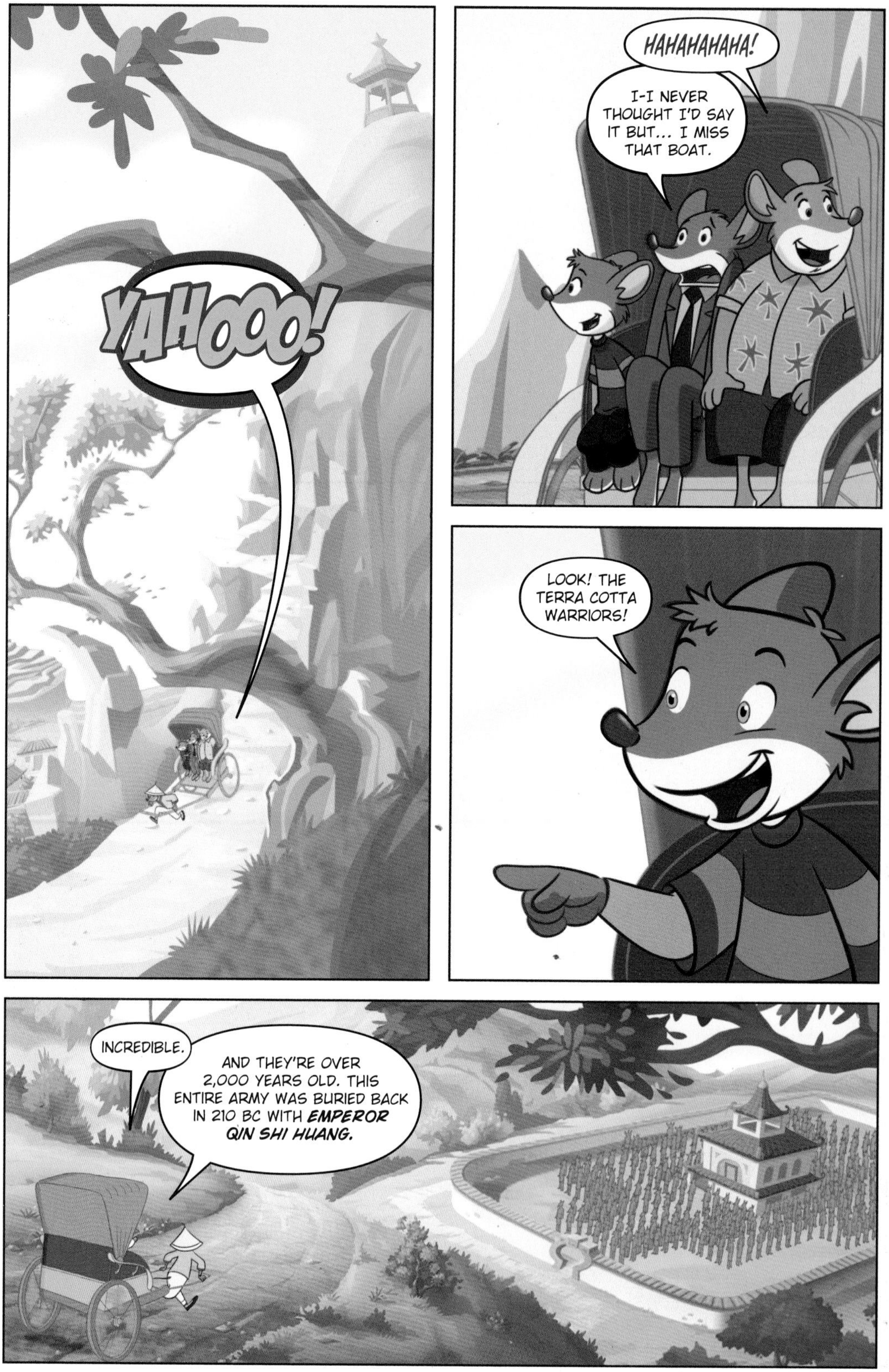
YAHOOO!
HAHAHAHAHA!
I-I NEVER THOUGHT I'D SAY IT BUT... I MISS THAT BOAT.
LOOK! THE TERRA COTTA WARRIORS!
INCREDIBLE.
AND THEY'RE OVER 2,000 YEARS OLD. THIS ENTIRE ARMY WAS BURIED BACK IN 210 BC WITH EMPEROR QIN SHI HUANG.

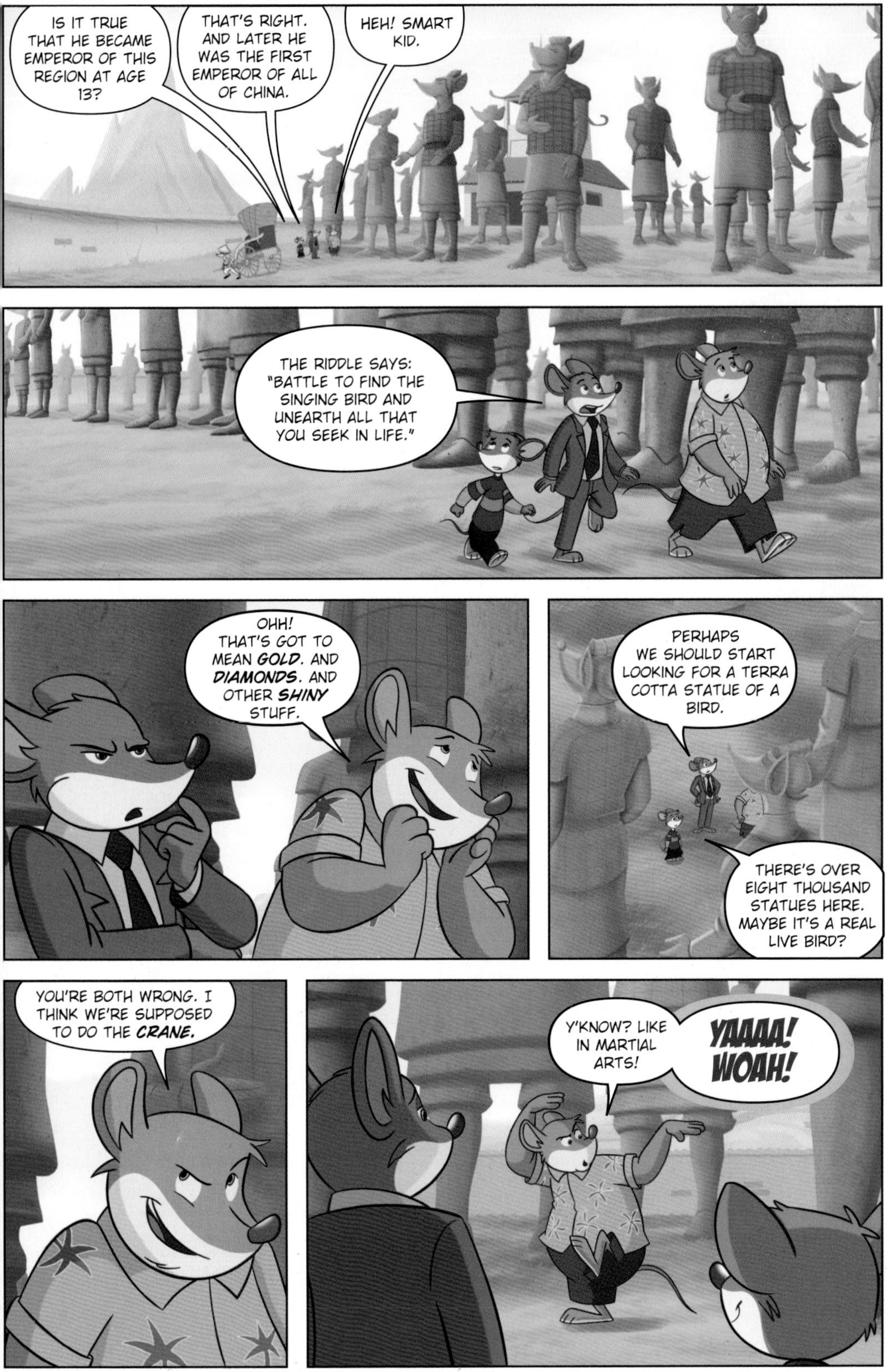
IS IT TRUE THAT HE BECAME EMPEROR OF THIS REGION AT AGE 13?
THAT'S RIGHT. AND LATER HE WAS THE FIRST EMPEROR OF ALL OF CHINA.
HEH! SMART KID.
THE RIDDLE SAYS: "BATTLE TO FIND THE SINGING BIRD AND UNEARTH ALL THAT YOU SEEK IN LIFE."
OHH! THAT'S GOT TO MEAN GOLD. AND DIAMONDS. AND OTHER SHINY STUFF.
PERHAPS WE SHOULD START LOOKING FOR A TERRA COTTA STATUE OF A BIRD.
THERE'S OVER EIGHT THOUSAND STATUES HERE. MAYBE IT'S A REAL LIVE BIRD?
YOU'RE BOTH WRONG. I THINK WE'RE SUPPOSED TO DO THE CRANE.
Y'KNOW? LIKE IN MARTIAL ARTS!
YAAAA! WOAH!

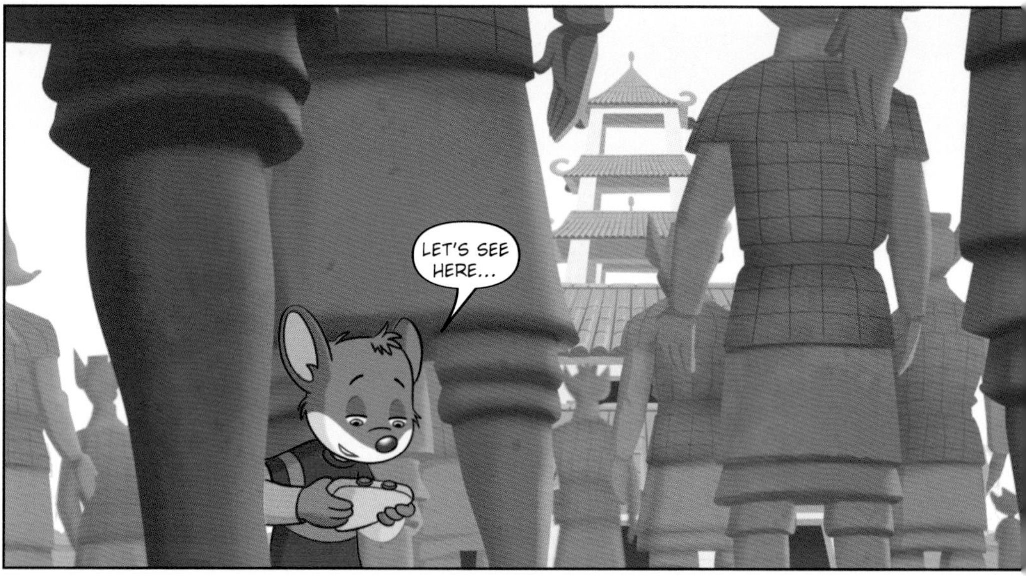
LET'S SEE HERE...

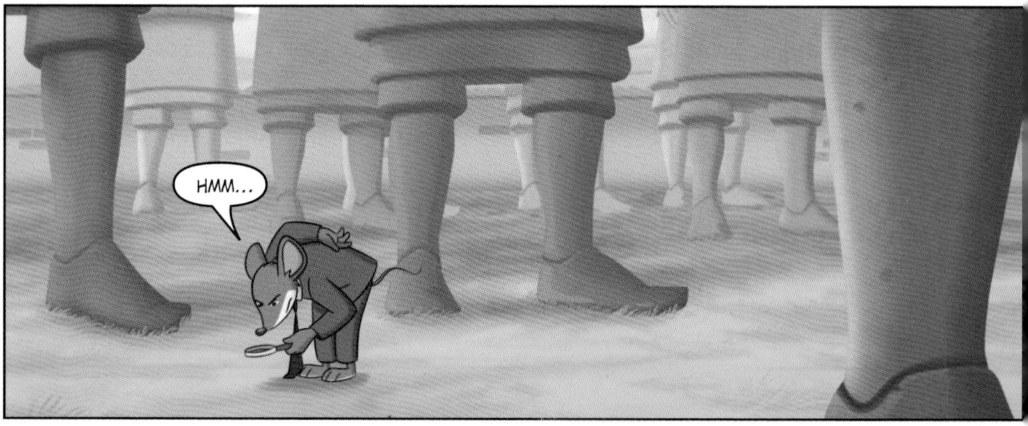
HMM...

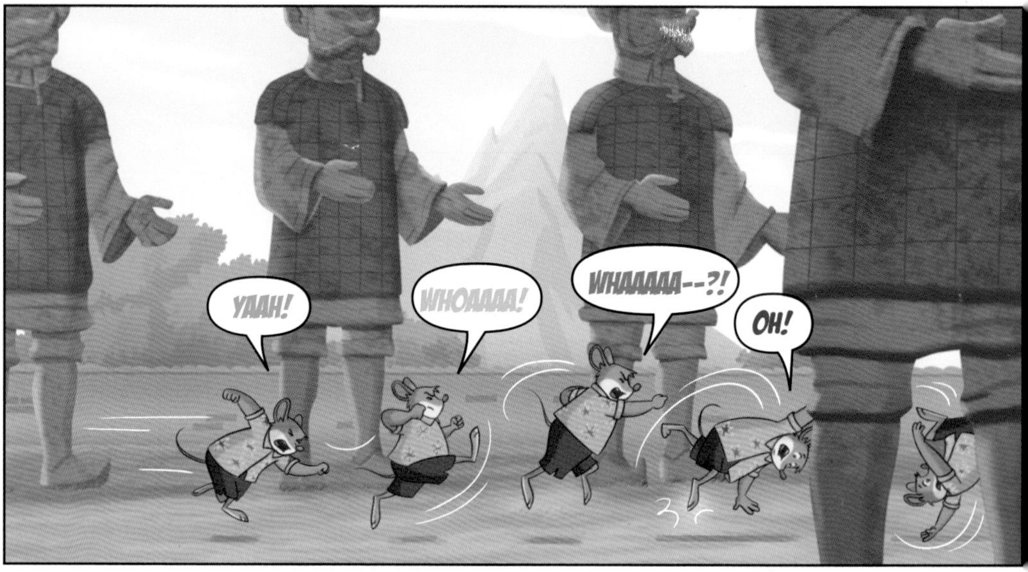
YAAH!
WHOAAAA!
WHAAAAA--?!
OH!

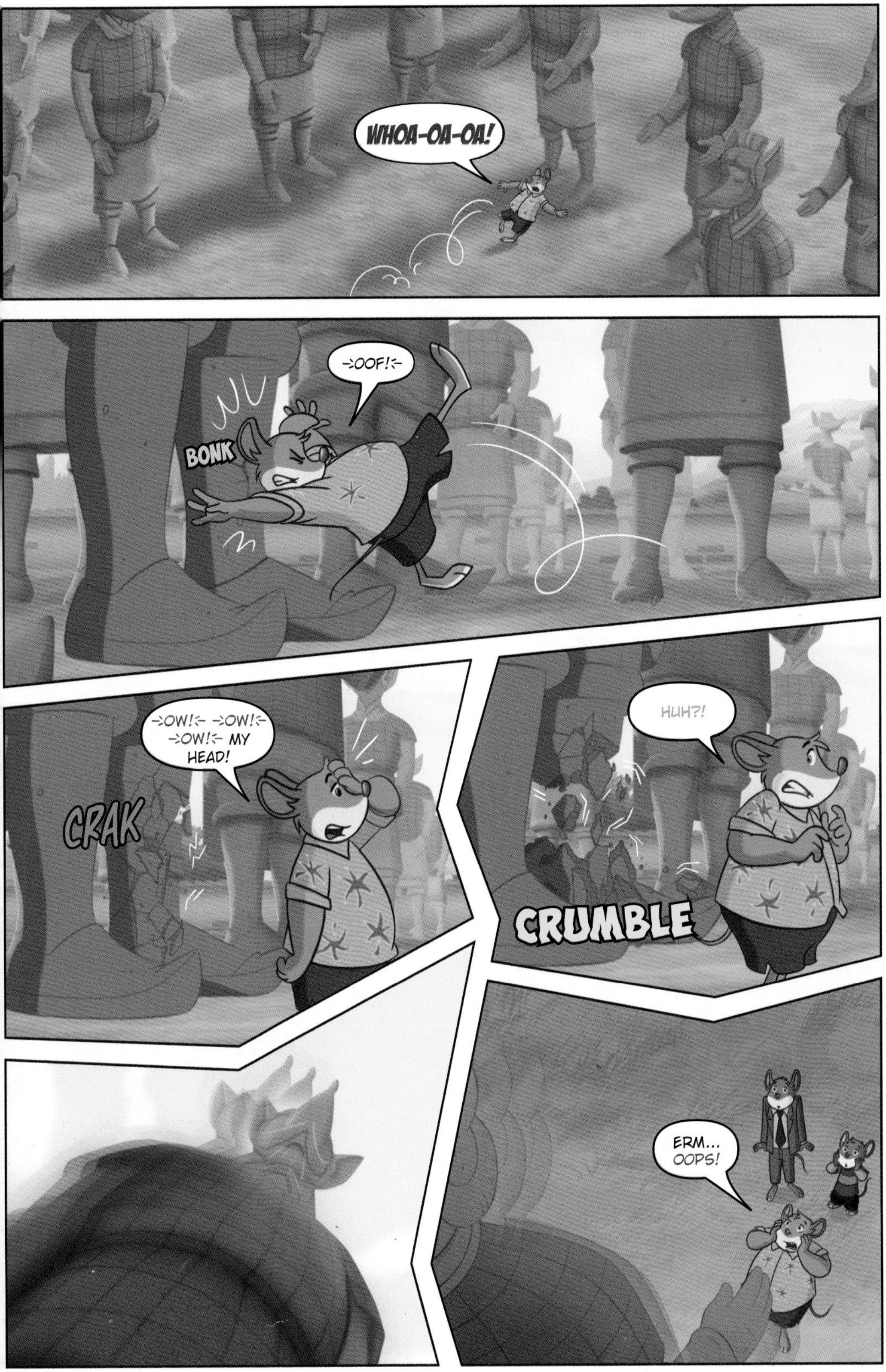
WHOA-OA-OA!
BONK
-OOF!-
-OW!- -OW!- -OW!- MY HEAD!
CRAK
HUH?!
CRUMBLE
ERM... OOPS!

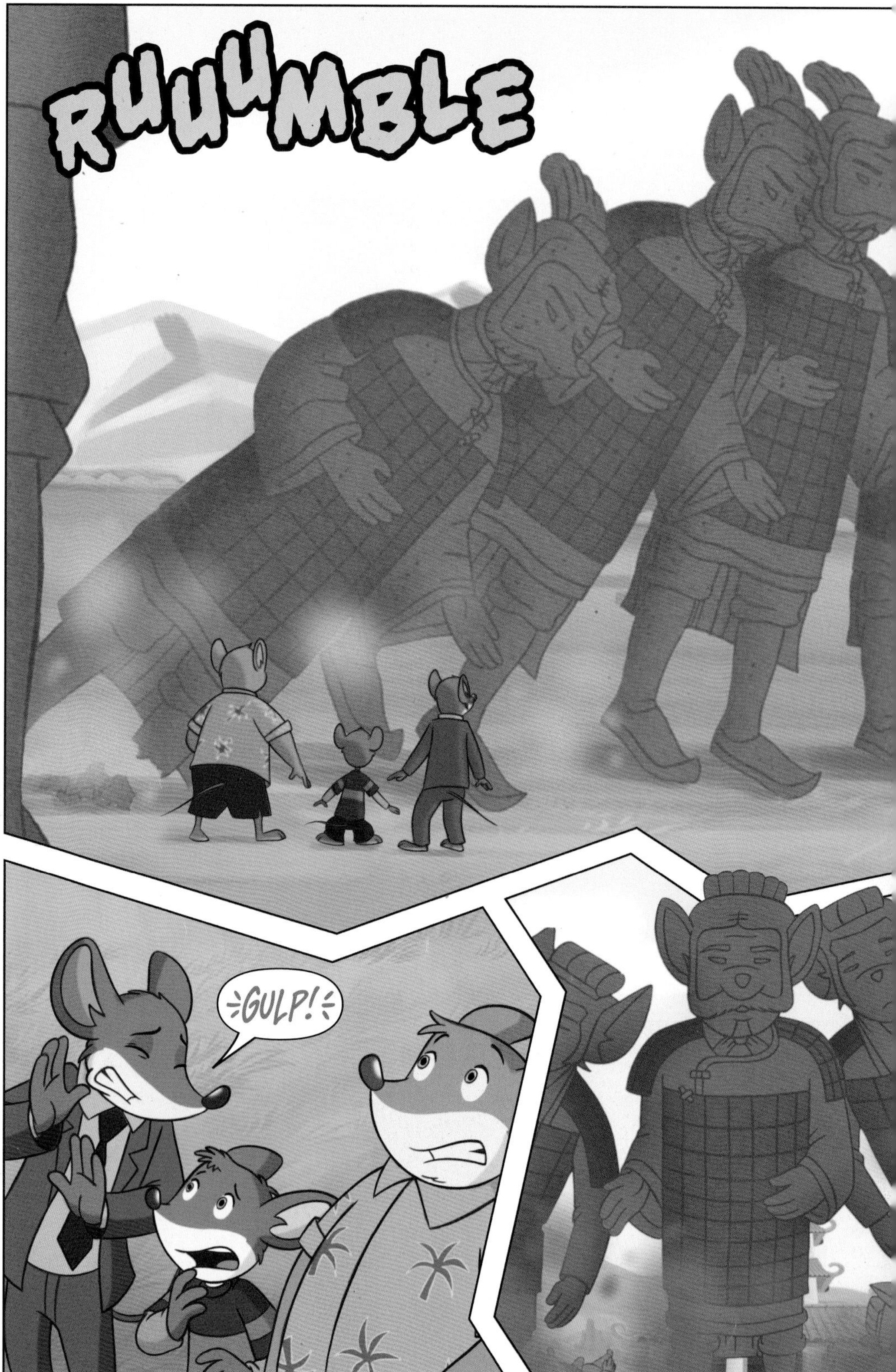
RUUUMBLE
GULP!

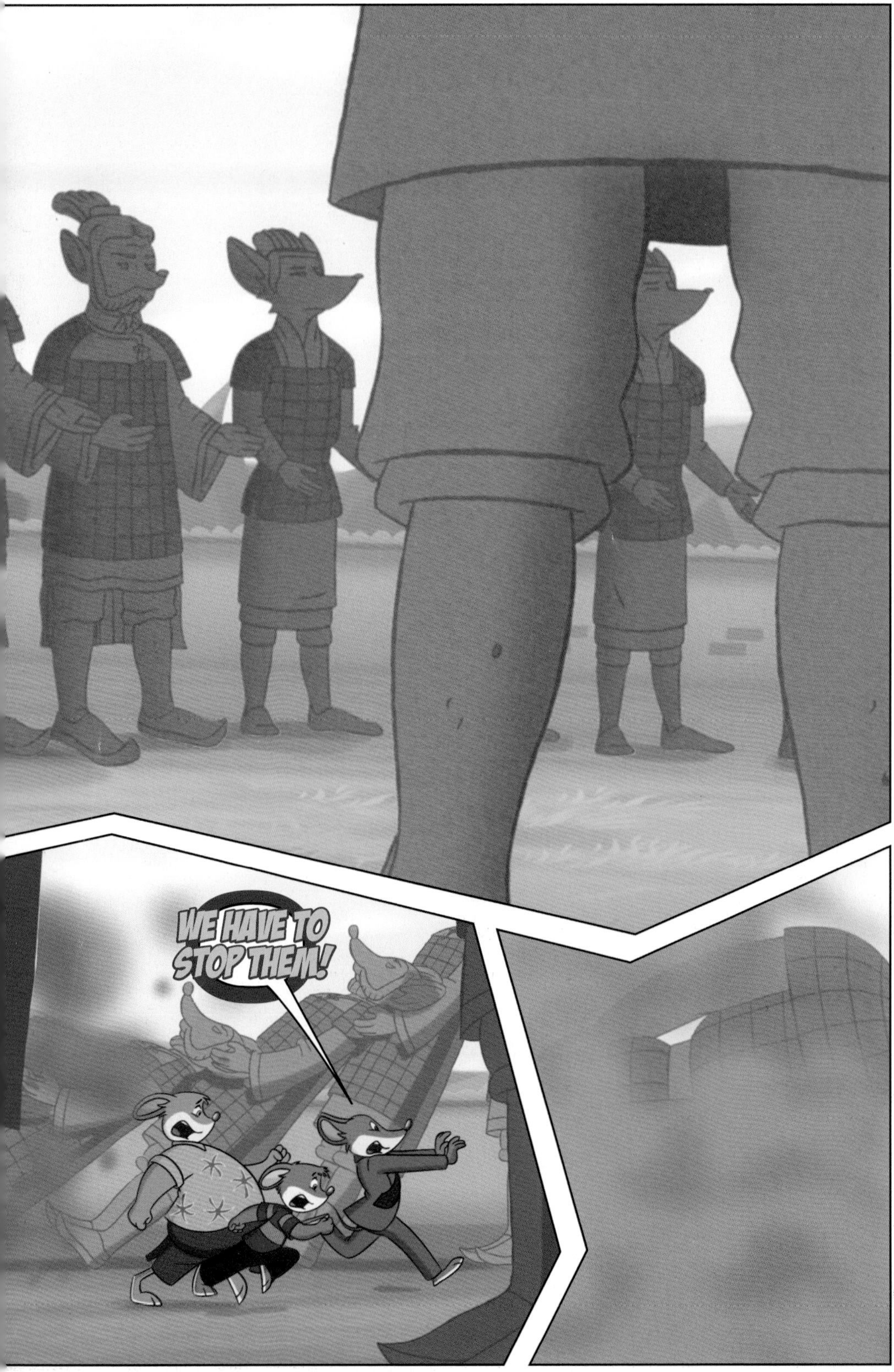
WE HAVE TO STOP THEM!

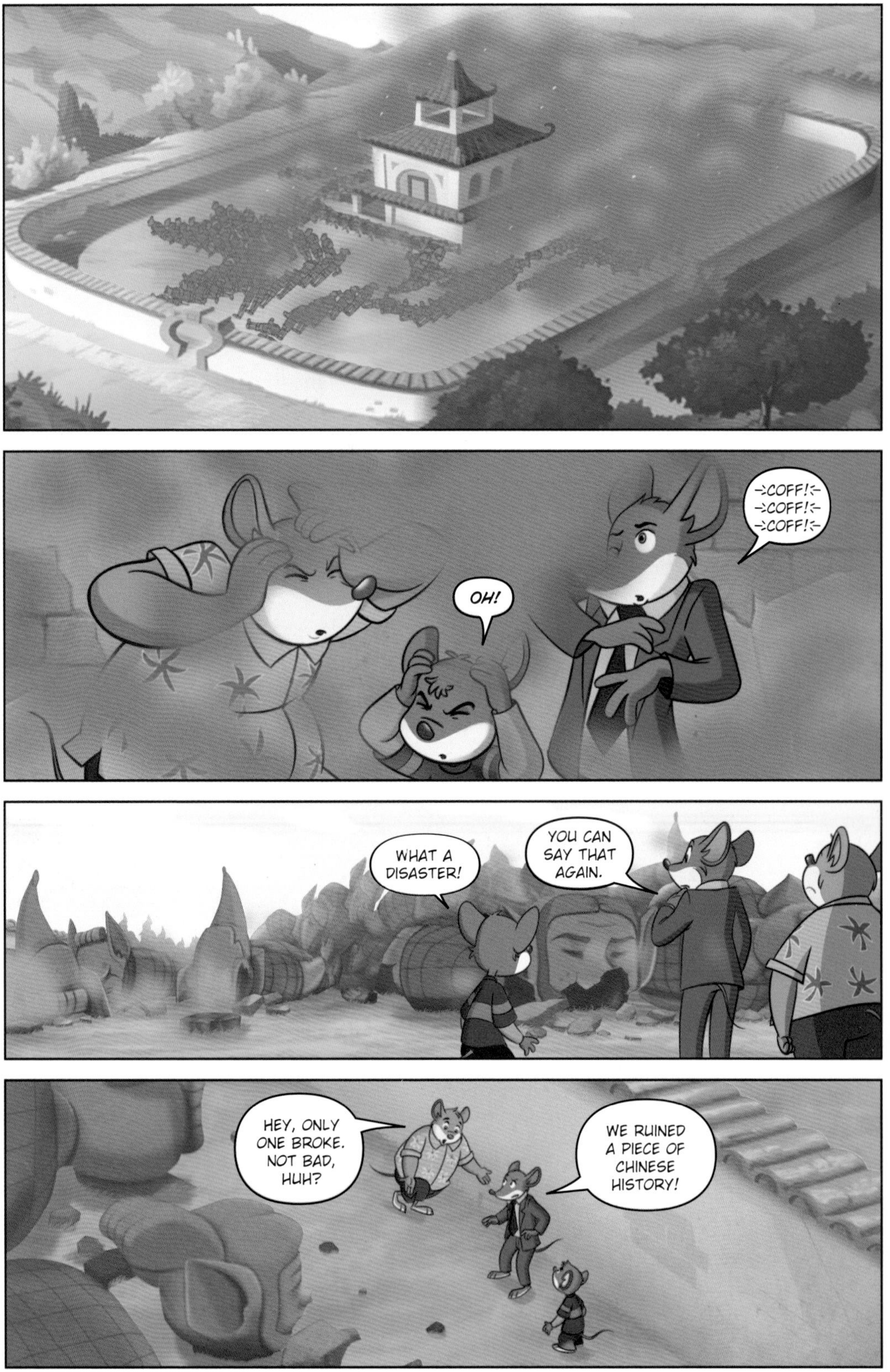
OH!
COFF! COFF! COFF!
WHAT A DISASTER!
YOU CAN SAY THAT AGAIN.
HEY, ONLY ONE BROKE. NOT BAD, HUH?
WE RUINED A PIECE OF CHINESE HISTORY!

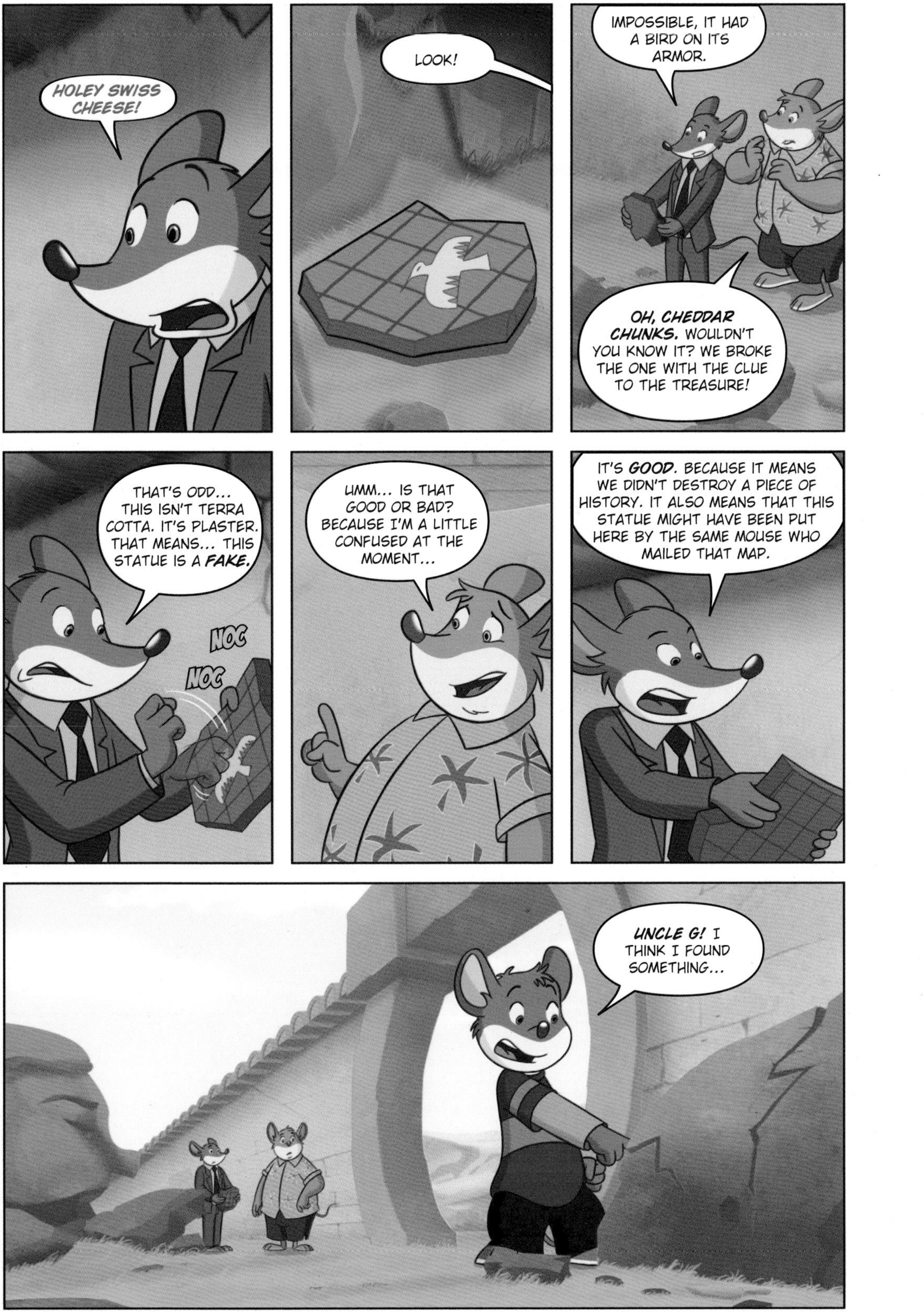
HOLEY SWISS CHEESE!
LOOK!
IMPOSSIBLE, IT HAD A BIRD ON ITS ARMOR.
OH, CHEDDAR CHUNKS. WOULDN'T YOU KNOW IT? WE BROKE THE ONE WITH THE CLUE TO THE TREASURE!
THAT'S ODD... THIS ISN'T TERRA COTTA. IT'S PLASTER. THAT MEANS... THIS STATUE IS A FAKE.
NOC
NOC
UMM... IS THAT GOOD OR BAD? BECAUSE I'M A LITTLE CONFUSED AT THE MOMENT...
IT'S GOOD. BECAUSE IT MEANS WE DIDN'T DESTROY A PIECE OF HISTORY. IT ALSO MEANS THAT THIS STATUE MIGHT HAVE BEEN PUT HERE BY THE SAME MOUSE WHO MAILED THAT MAP.
UNCLE G! I THINK I FOUND SOMETHING...

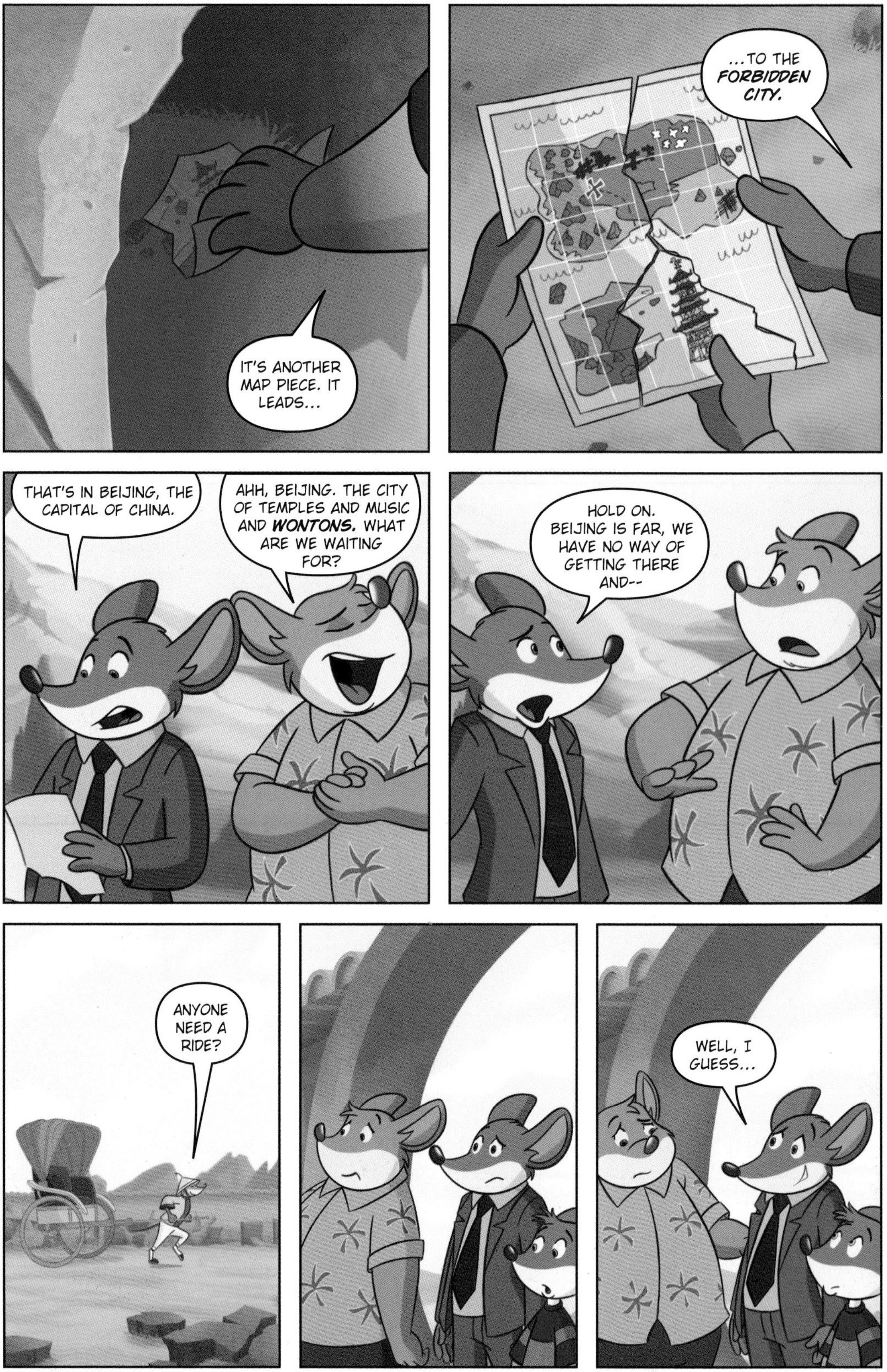
IT'S ANOTHER MAP PIECE. IT LEADS...
...TO THE FORBIDDEN CITY.
THAT'S IN BEIJING, THE CAPITAL OF CHINA.
AHH, BEIJING. THE CITY OF TEMPLES AND MUSIC AND WONTONS. WHAT ARE WE WAITING FOR?
HOLD ON. BEIJING IS FAR, WE HAVE NO WAY OF GETTING THERE AND--
ANYONE NEED A RIDE?
WELL, I GUESS...

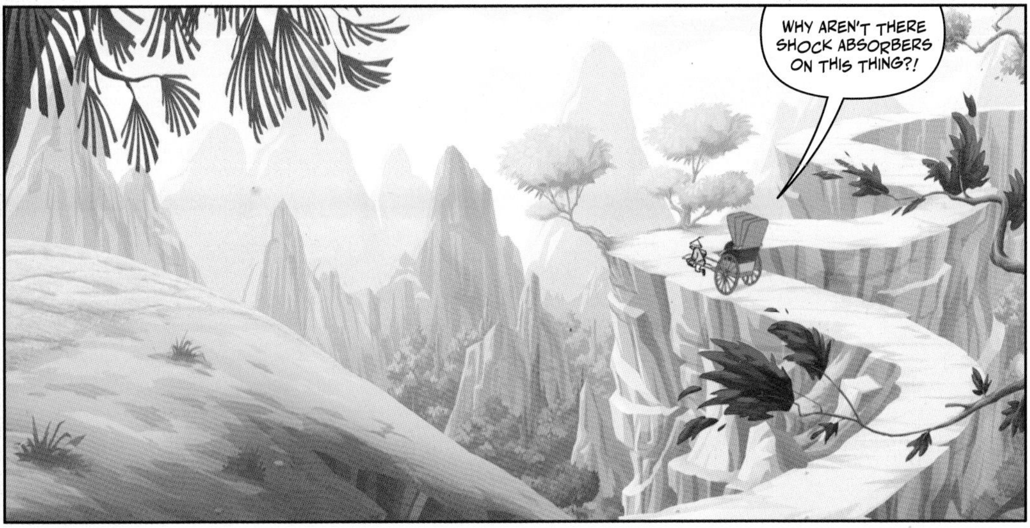
WHY AREN'T THERE SHOCK ABSORBERS ON THIS THING?!

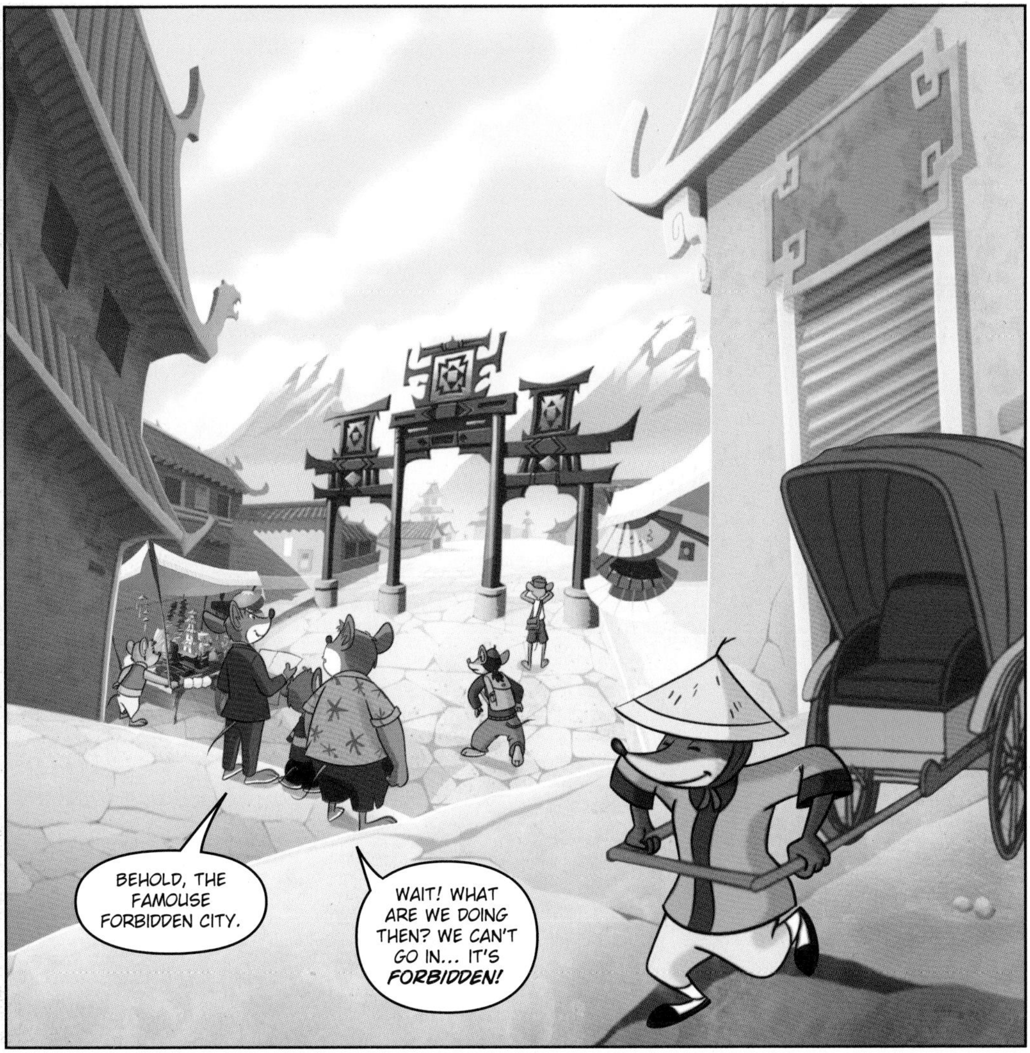
BEHOLD, THE FAMOUSE FORBIDDEN CITY.
WAIT! WHAT ARE WE DOING THEN? WE CAN'T GO IN... IT'S ***FORBIDDEN!***

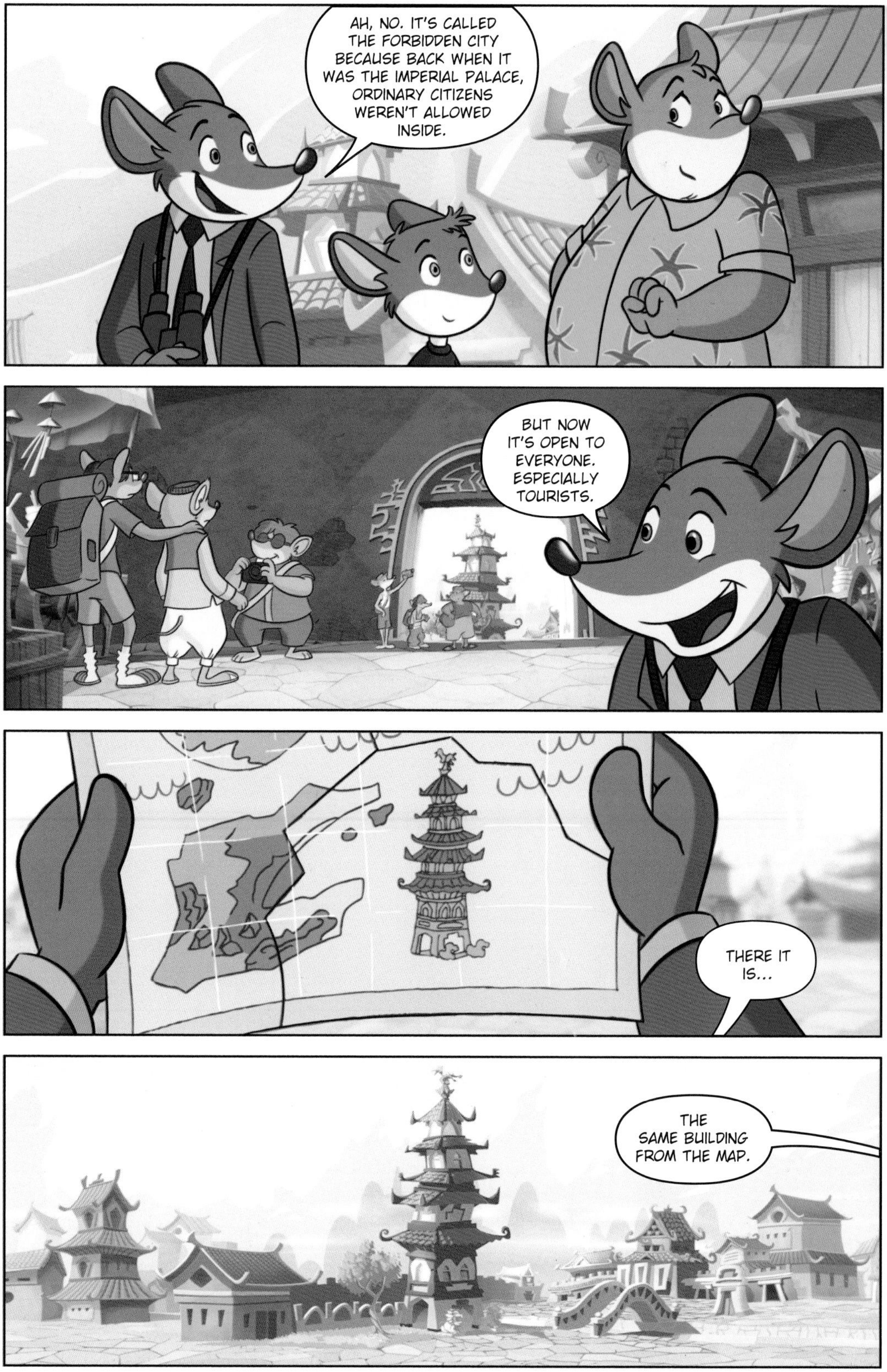
AH, NO. IT'S CALLED THE FORBIDDEN CITY BECAUSE BACK WHEN IT WAS THE IMPERIAL PALACE, ORDINARY CITIZENS WEREN'T ALLOWED INSIDE.
BUT NOW IT'S OPEN TO EVERYONE. ESPECIALLY TOURISTS.
THERE IT IS...
THE SAME BUILDING FROM THE MAP.

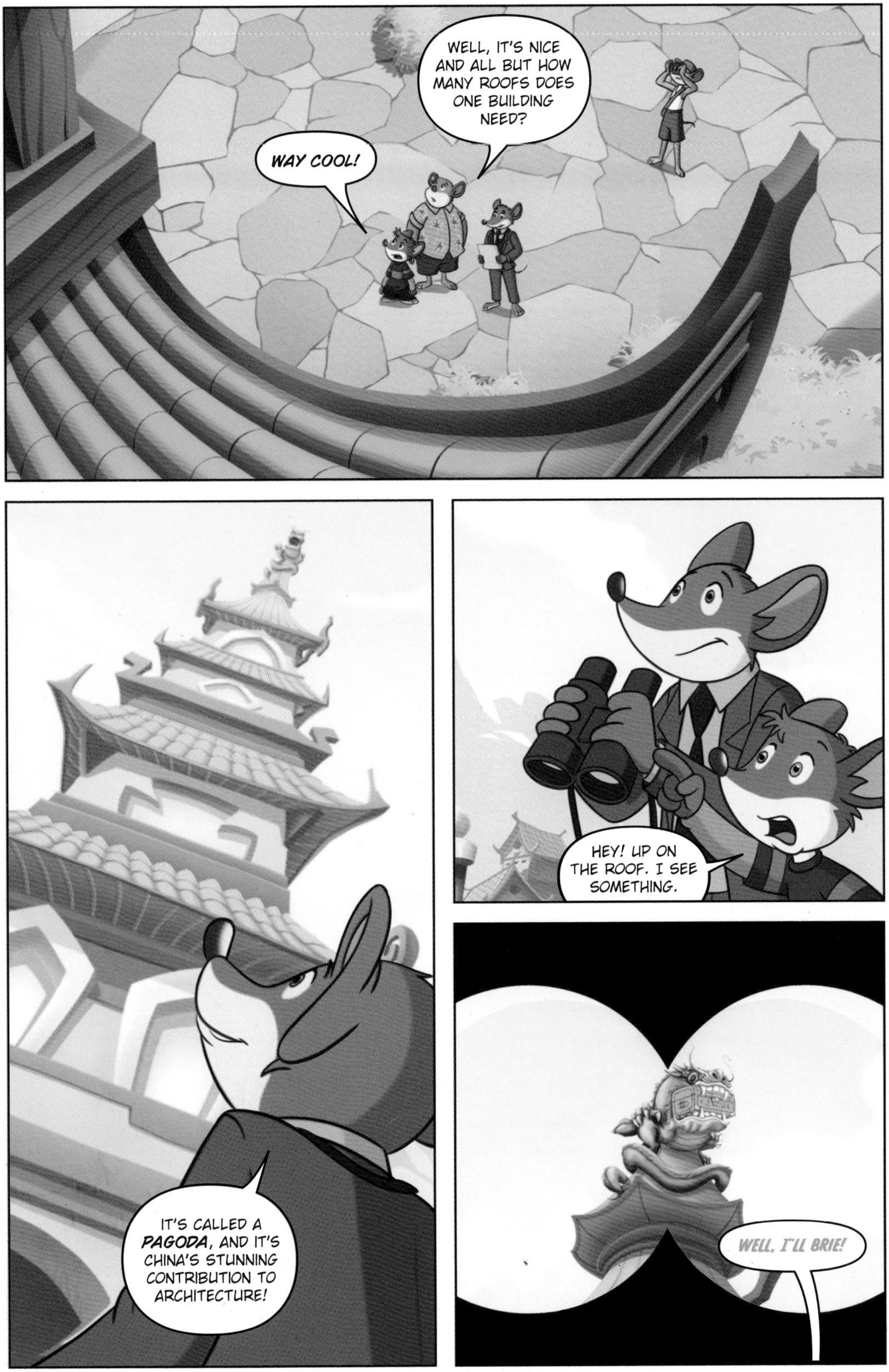
WAY COOL!
WELL, IT'S NICE AND ALL BUT HOW MANY ROOFS DOES ONE BUILDING NEED?
IT'S CALLED A *PAGODA*, AND IT'S CHINA'S STUNNING CONTRIBUTION TO ARCHITECTURE!
HEY! UP ON THE ROOF. I SEE SOMETHING.
WELL, I'LL BRIE!

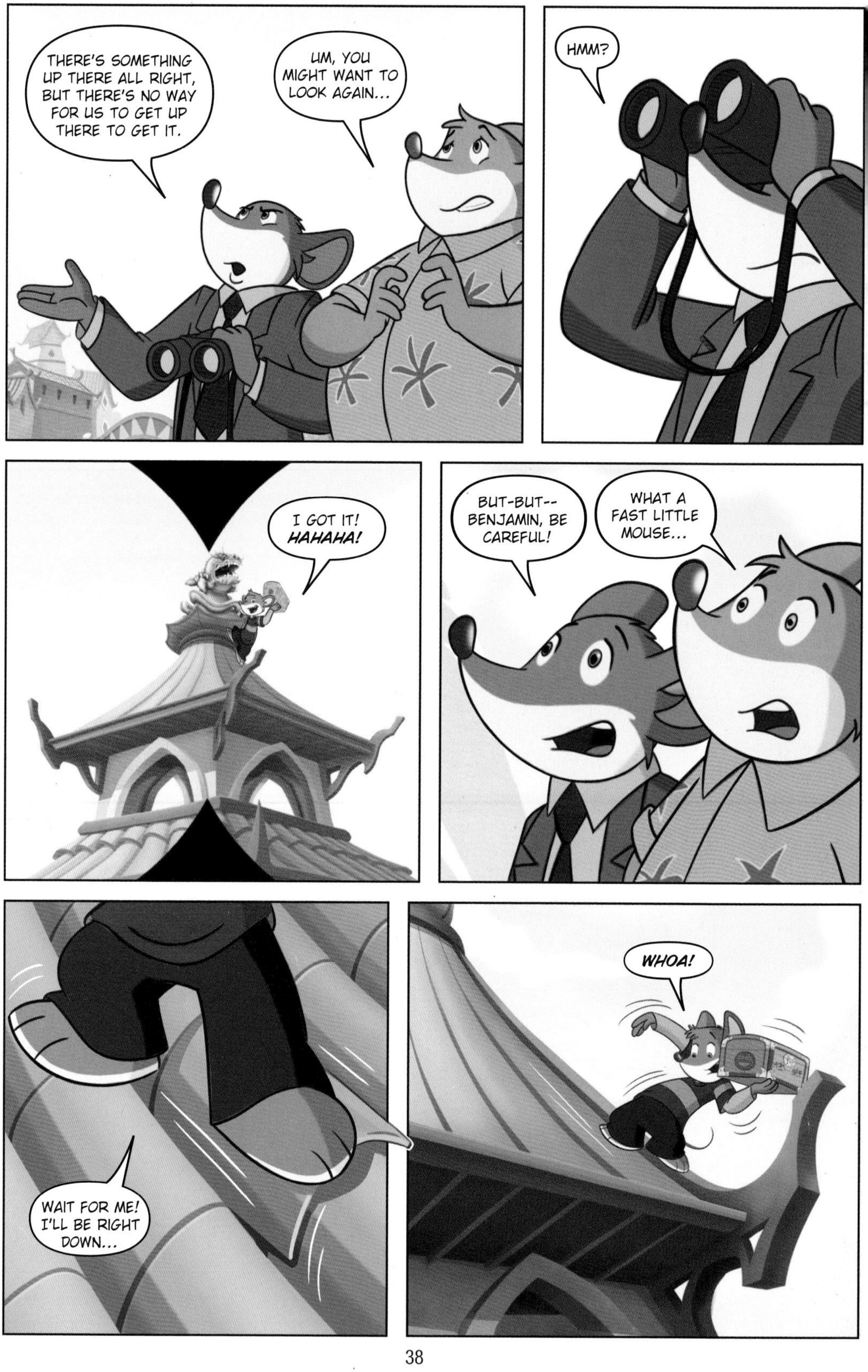
THERE'S SOMETHING UP THERE ALL RIGHT, BUT THERE'S NO WAY FOR US TO GET UP THERE TO GET IT.
UM, YOU MIGHT WANT TO LOOK AGAIN...
HMM?
I GOT IT! HAHAHA!
BUT-BUT-- BENJAMIN, BE CAREFUL!
WHAT A FAST LITTLE MOUSE...
WAIT FOR ME! I'LL BE RIGHT DOWN...
WHOA!

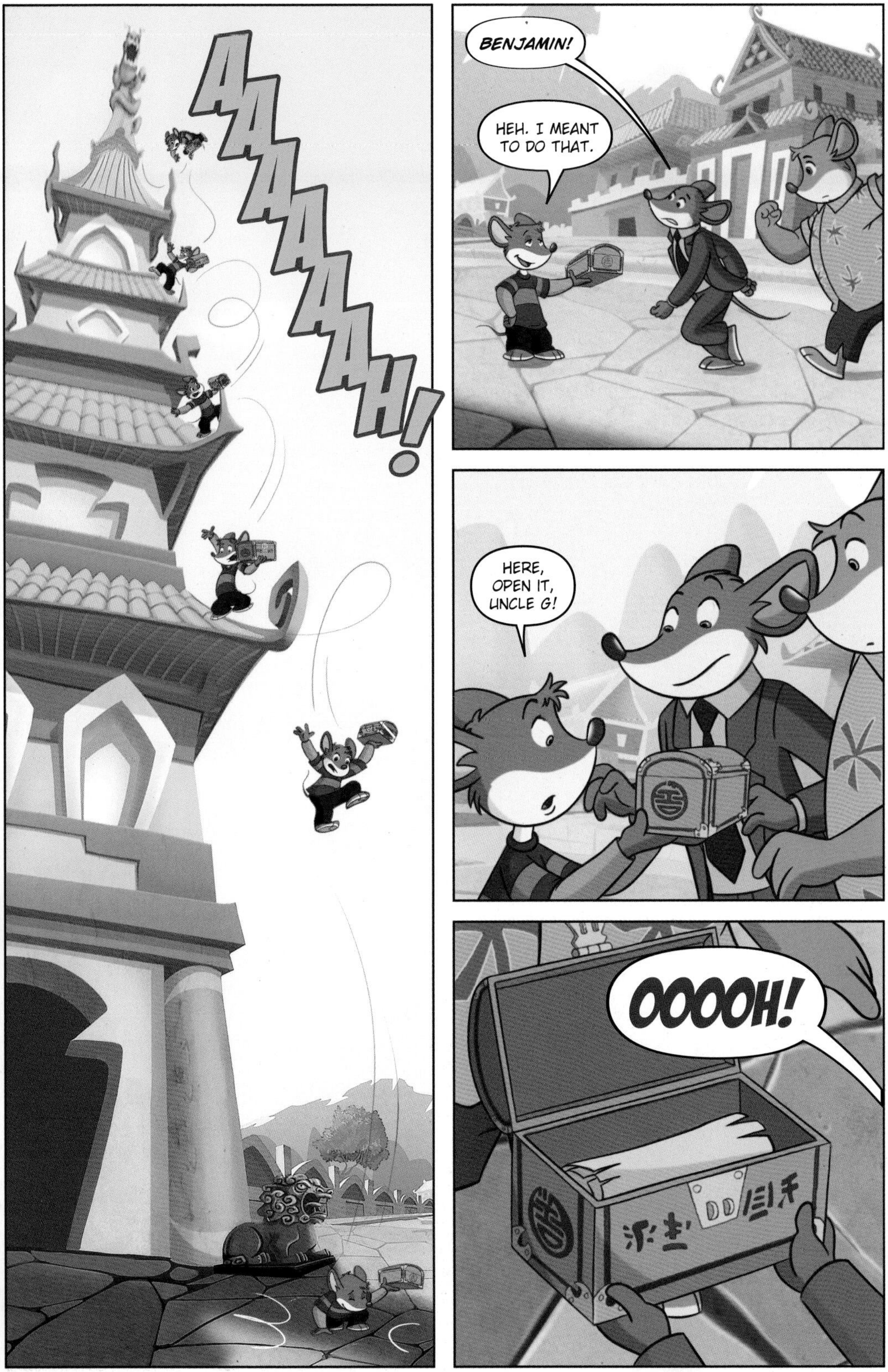
AAAAAAAAAH!
BENJAMIN!
HEH. I MEANT TO DO THAT.
HERE, OPEN IT, UNCLE G!
OOOOH!

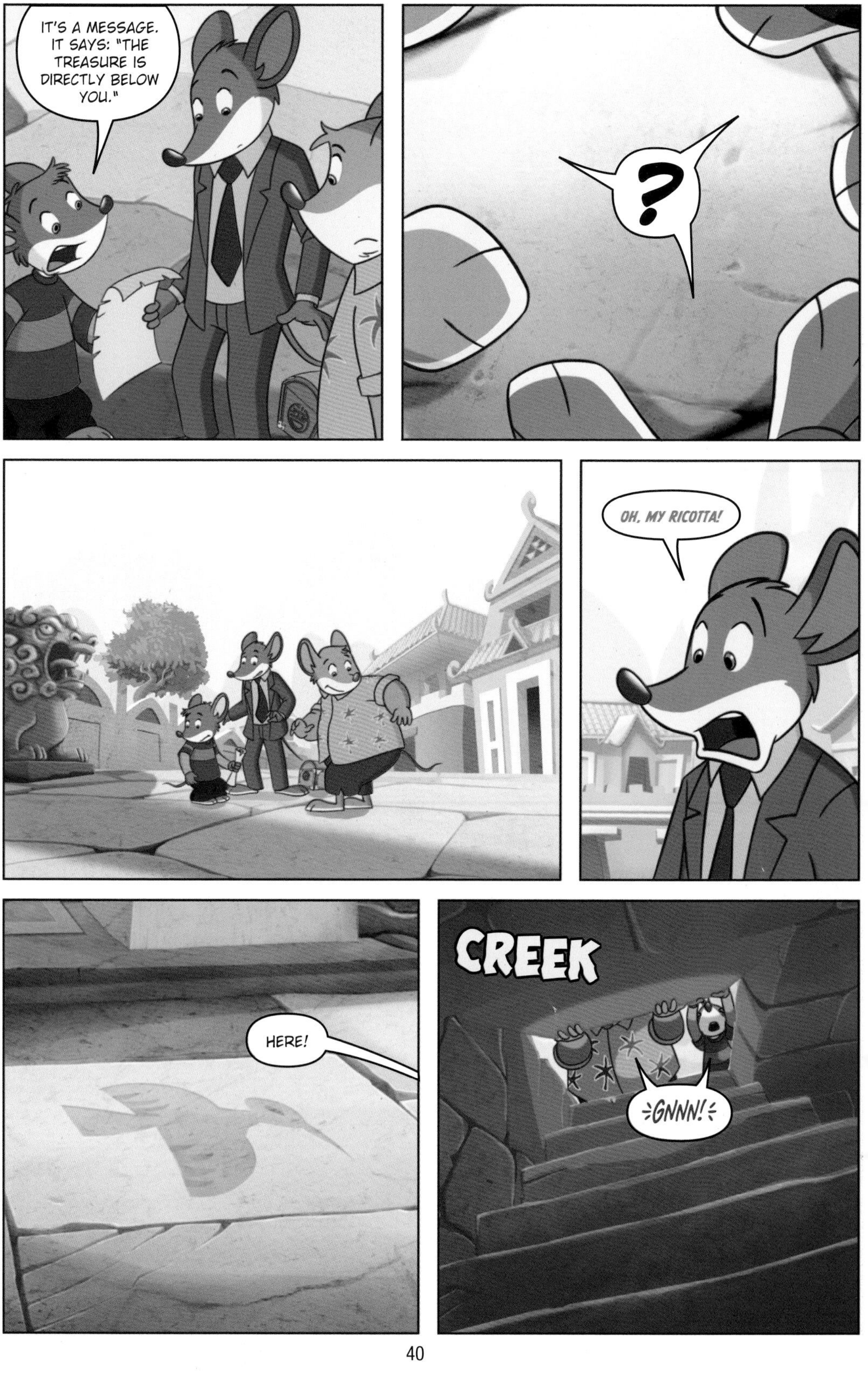
IT'S A MESSAGE. IT SAYS: "THE TREASURE IS DIRECTLY BELOW YOU."
?
OH, MY RICOTTA!
HERE!
CREEK
GNNN!

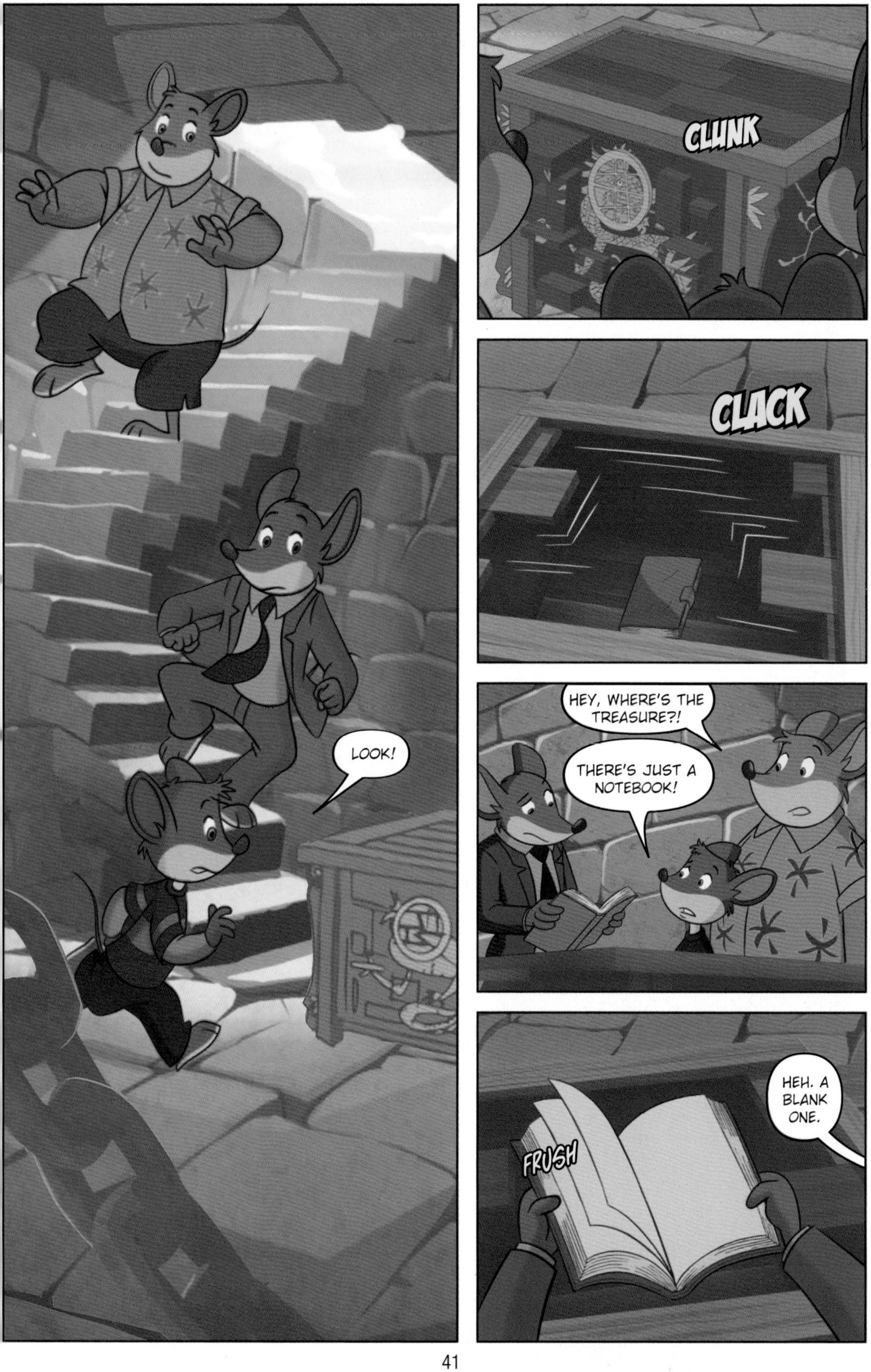
LOOK!
CLUNK
CLACK
HEY, WHERE'S THE TREASURE?!
THERE'S JUST A NOTEBOOK!
FRUSH
HEH. A BLANK ONE.

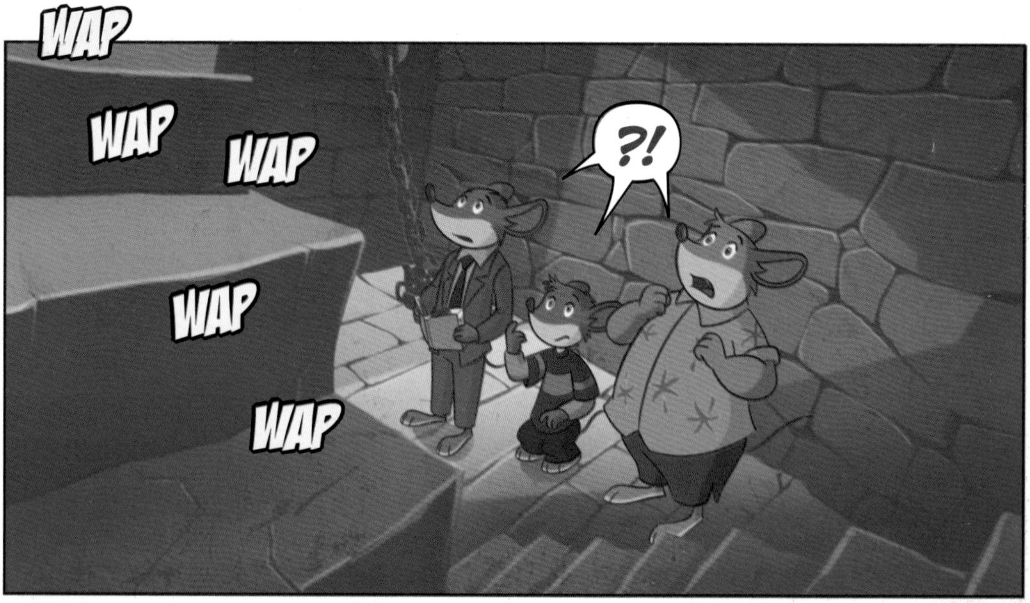
WAP
WAP
WAP
WAP
WAP
?!

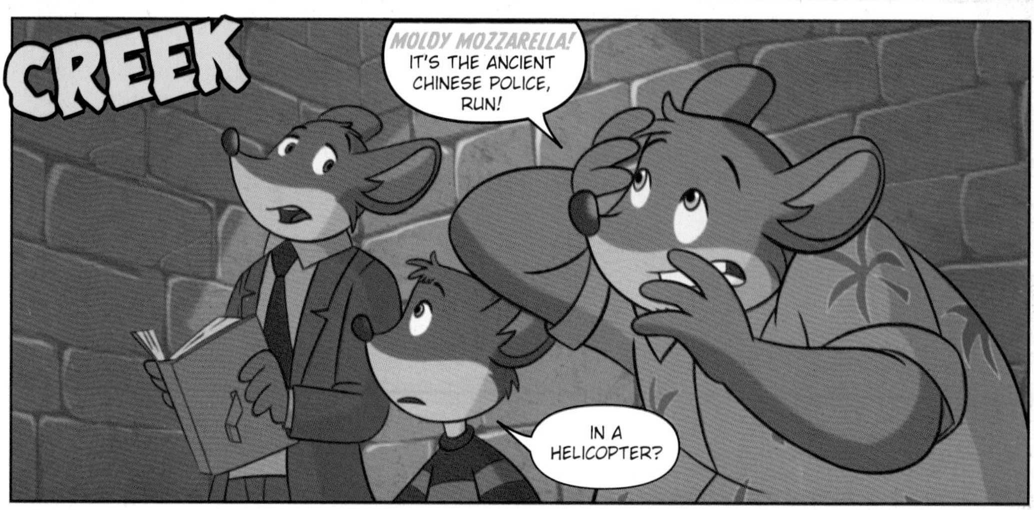
CREEK
MOLDY MOZZARELLA! IT'S THE ANCIENT CHINESE POLICE, RUN!
IN A HELICOPTER?

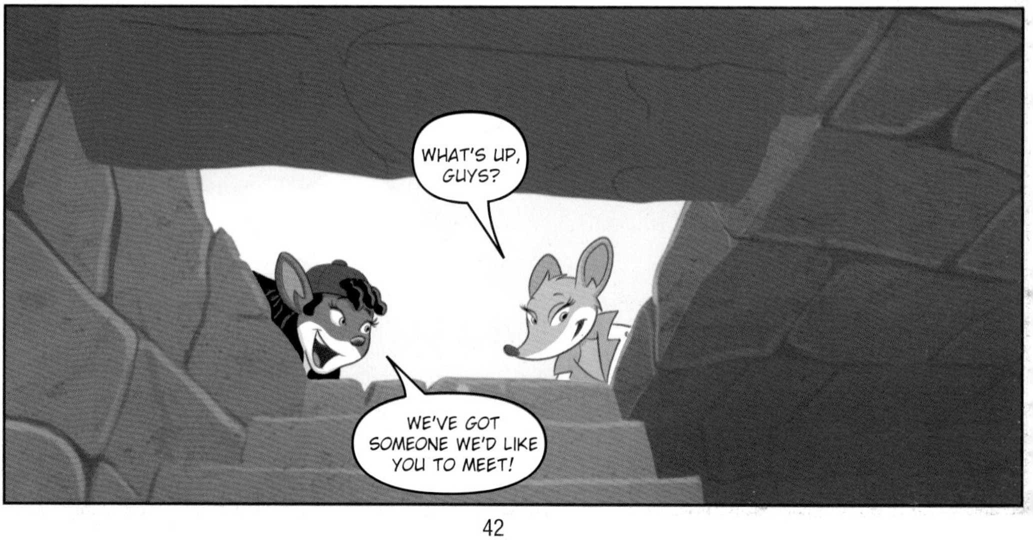
WHAT'S UP, GUYS?
WE'VE GOT SOMEONE WE'D LIKE YOU TO MEET!

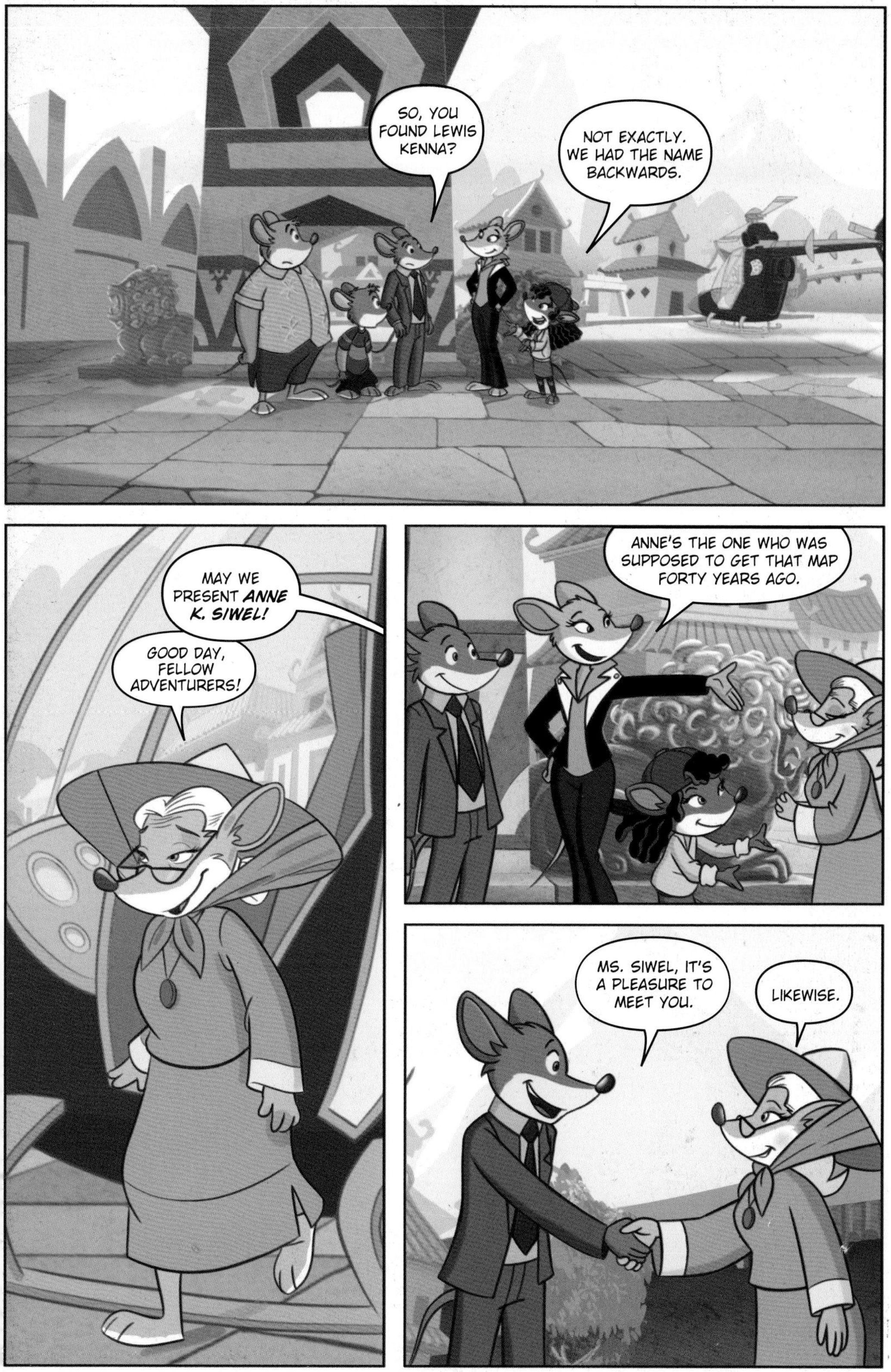
SO, YOU FOUND LEWIS KENNA?
NOT EXACTLY. WE HAD THE NAME BACKWARDS.
MAY WE PRESENT ANNE K. SIWEL!
GOOD DAY, FELLOW ADVENTURERS!
ANNE'S THE ONE WHO WAS SUPPOSED TO GET THAT MAP FORTY YEARS AGO.
MS. SIWEL, IT'S A PLEASURE TO MEET YOU.
LIKEWISE.

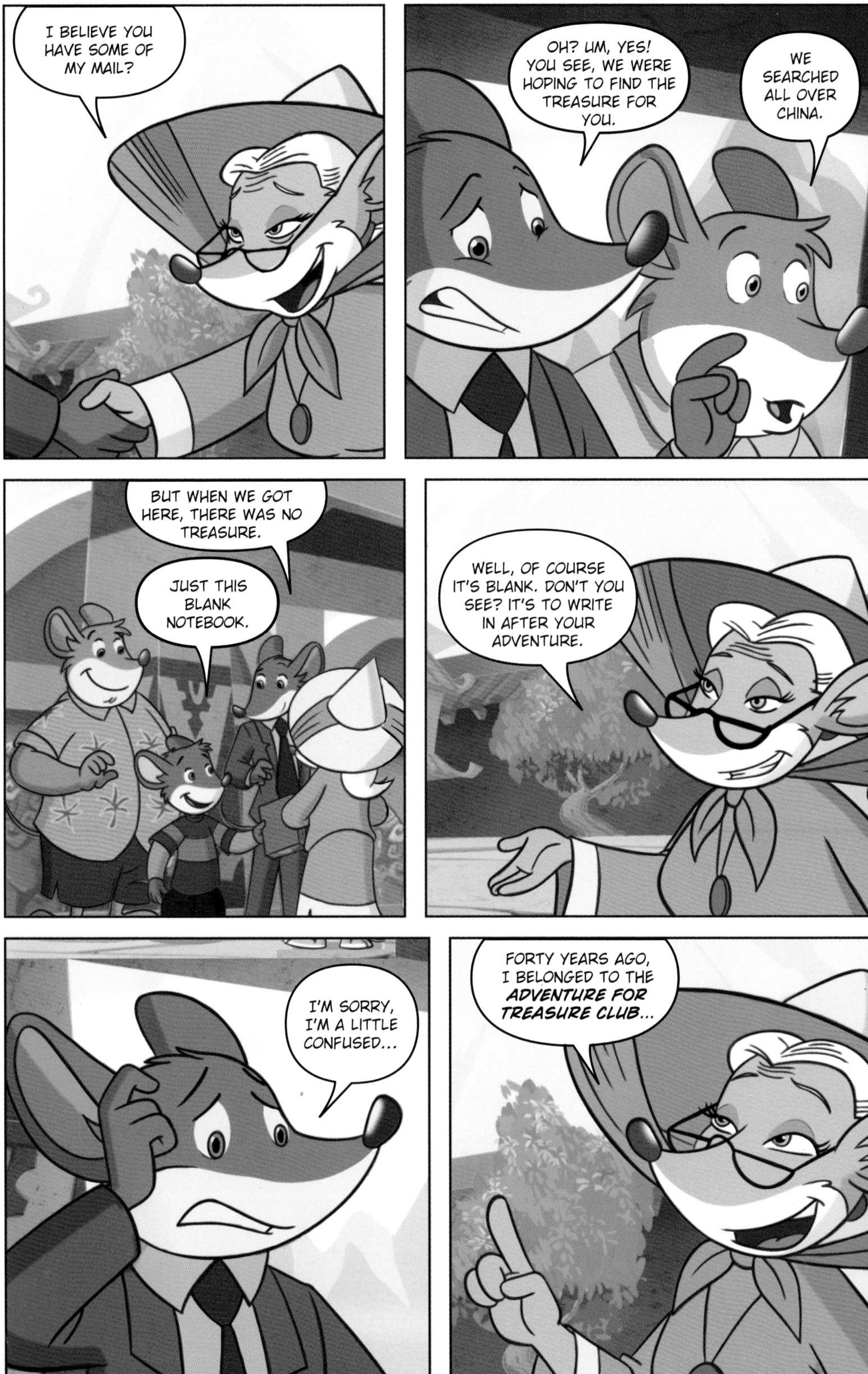
I BELIEVE YOU HAVE SOME OF MY MAIL?
OH? UM, YES! YOU SEE, WE WERE HOPING TO FIND THE TREASURE FOR YOU.
WE SEARCHED ALL OVER CHINA.
BUT WHEN WE GOT HERE, THERE WAS NO TREASURE.
JUST THIS BLANK NOTEBOOK.
WELL, OF COURSE IT'S BLANK. DON'T YOU SEE? IT'S TO WRITE IN AFTER YOUR ADVENTURE.
I'M SORRY, I'M A LITTLE CONFUSED...
FORTY YEARS AGO, I BELONGED TO THE ADVENTURE FOR TREASURE CLUB...

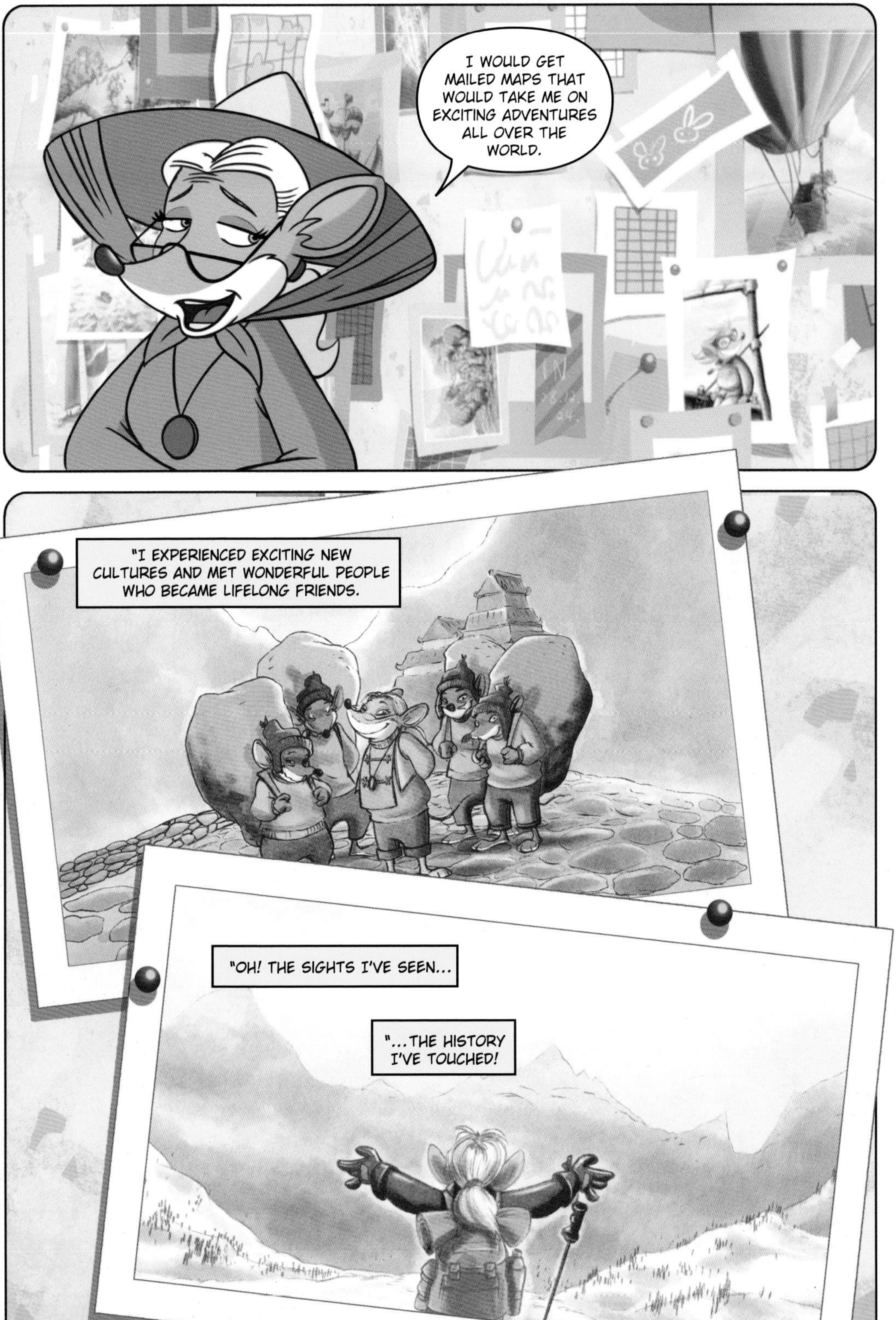
I WOULD GET MAILED MAPS THAT WOULD TAKE ME ON EXCITING ADVENTURES ALL OVER THE WORLD.
"I EXPERIENCED EXCITING NEW CULTURES AND MET WONDERFUL PEOPLE WHO BECAME LIFELONG FRIENDS.
"OH! THE SIGHTS I'VE SEEN...
"...THE HISTORY I'VE TOUCHED!

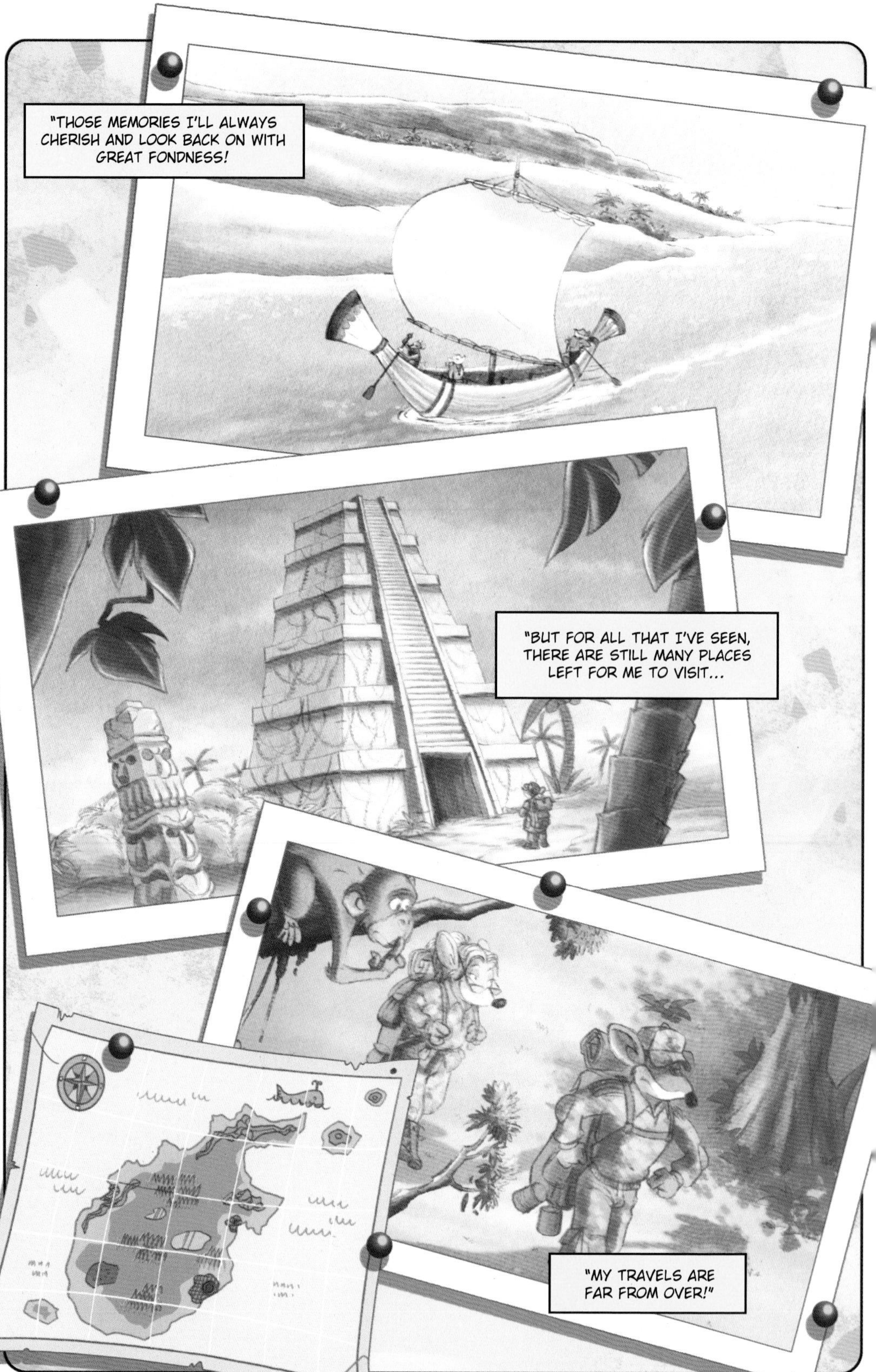
"THOSE MEMORIES I'LL ALWAYS CHERISH AND LOOK BACK ON WITH GREAT FONDNESS!
"BUT FOR ALL THAT I'VE SEEN, THERE ARE STILL MANY PLACES LEFT FOR ME TO VISIT...
"MY TRAVELS ARE FAR FROM OVER!"

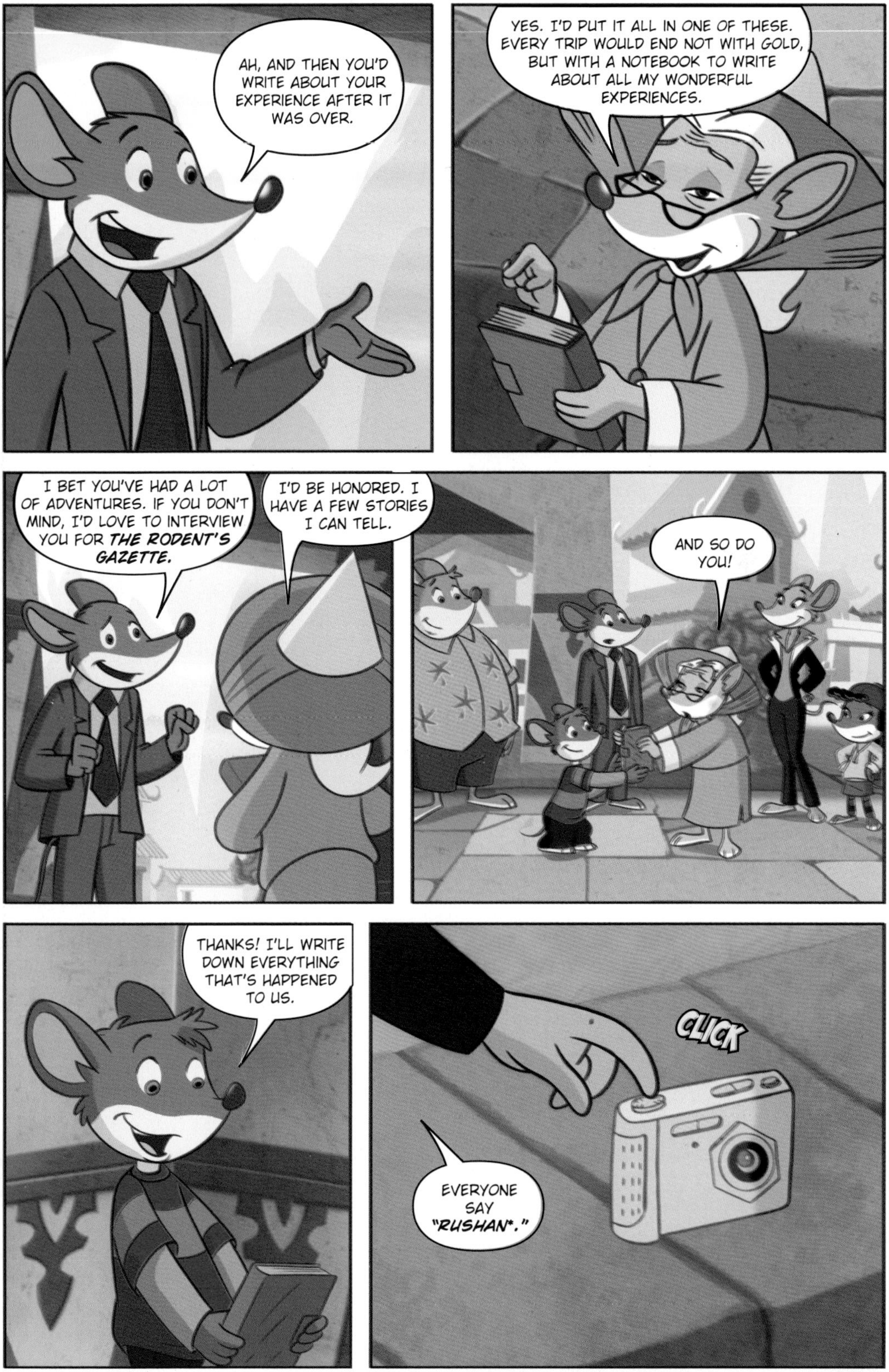
AH, AND THEN YOU'D WRITE ABOUT YOUR EXPERIENCE AFTER IT WAS OVER.
YES. I'D PUT IT ALL IN ONE OF THESE. EVERY TRIP WOULD END NOT WITH GOLD, BUT WITH A NOTEBOOK TO WRITE ABOUT ALL MY WONDERFUL EXPERIENCES.
I BET YOU'VE HAD A LOT OF ADVENTURES. IF YOU DON'T MIND, I'D LOVE TO INTERVIEW YOU FOR ***THE RODENT'S GAZETTE.***
I'D BE HONORED. I HAVE A FEW STORIES I CAN TELL.
AND SO DO YOU!
THANKS! I'LL WRITE DOWN EVERYTHING THAT'S HAPPENED TO US.
CLICK
EVERYONE SAY ***"RUSHAN*."***

***"RUSHAN CHEESE"** A TYPE OF CHINESE CHEESE MADE OF COWS' MILK CURDS WRAPPED AROUND BAMBOO STICKS.

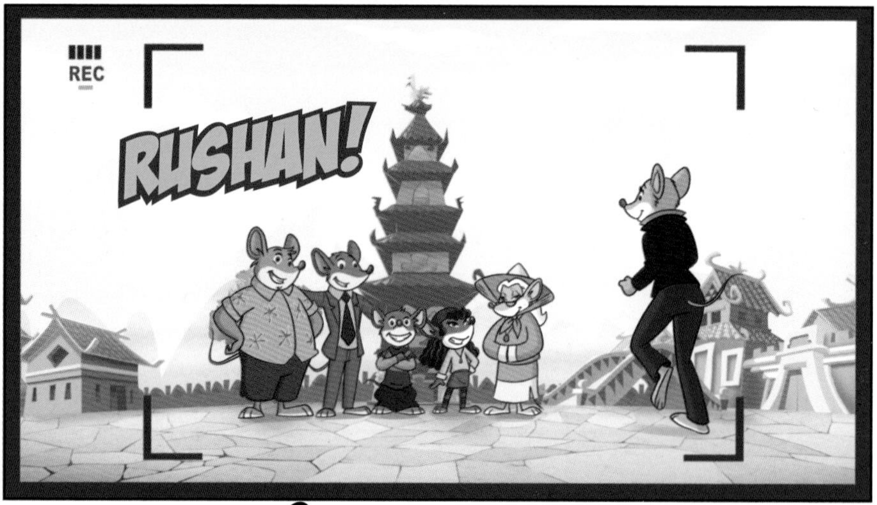
REC
RUSHAN!

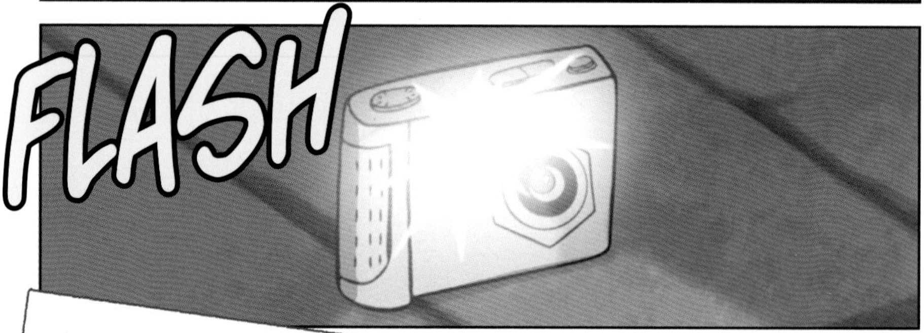
FLASH

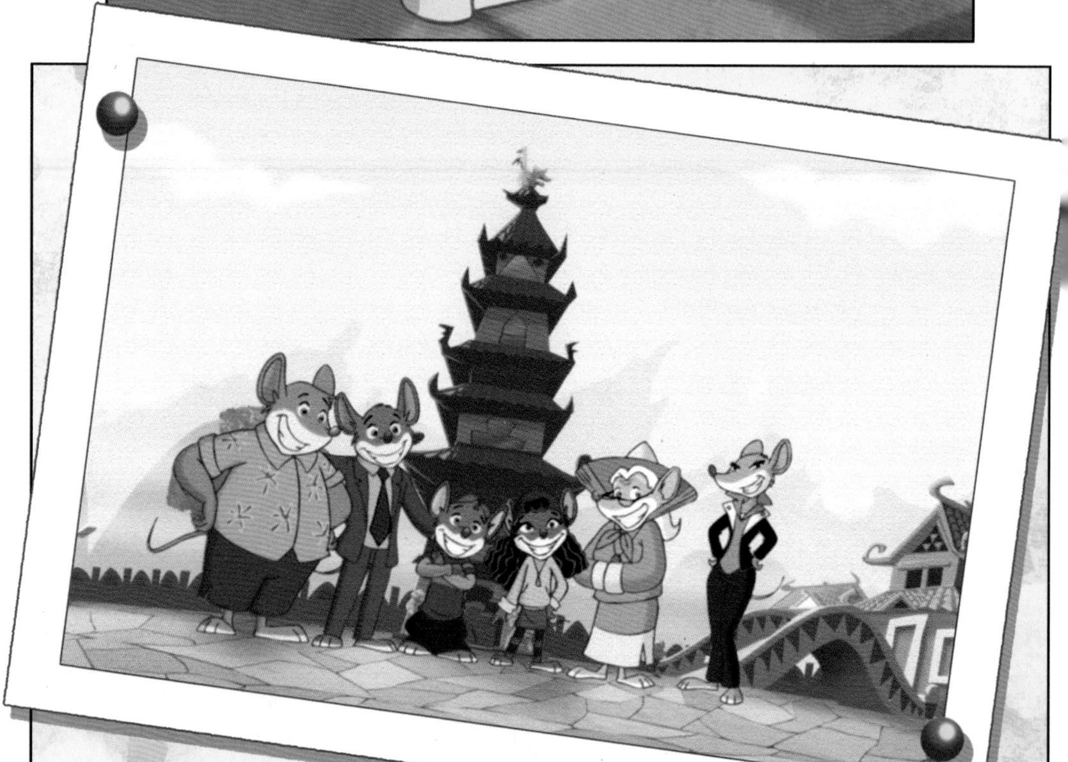

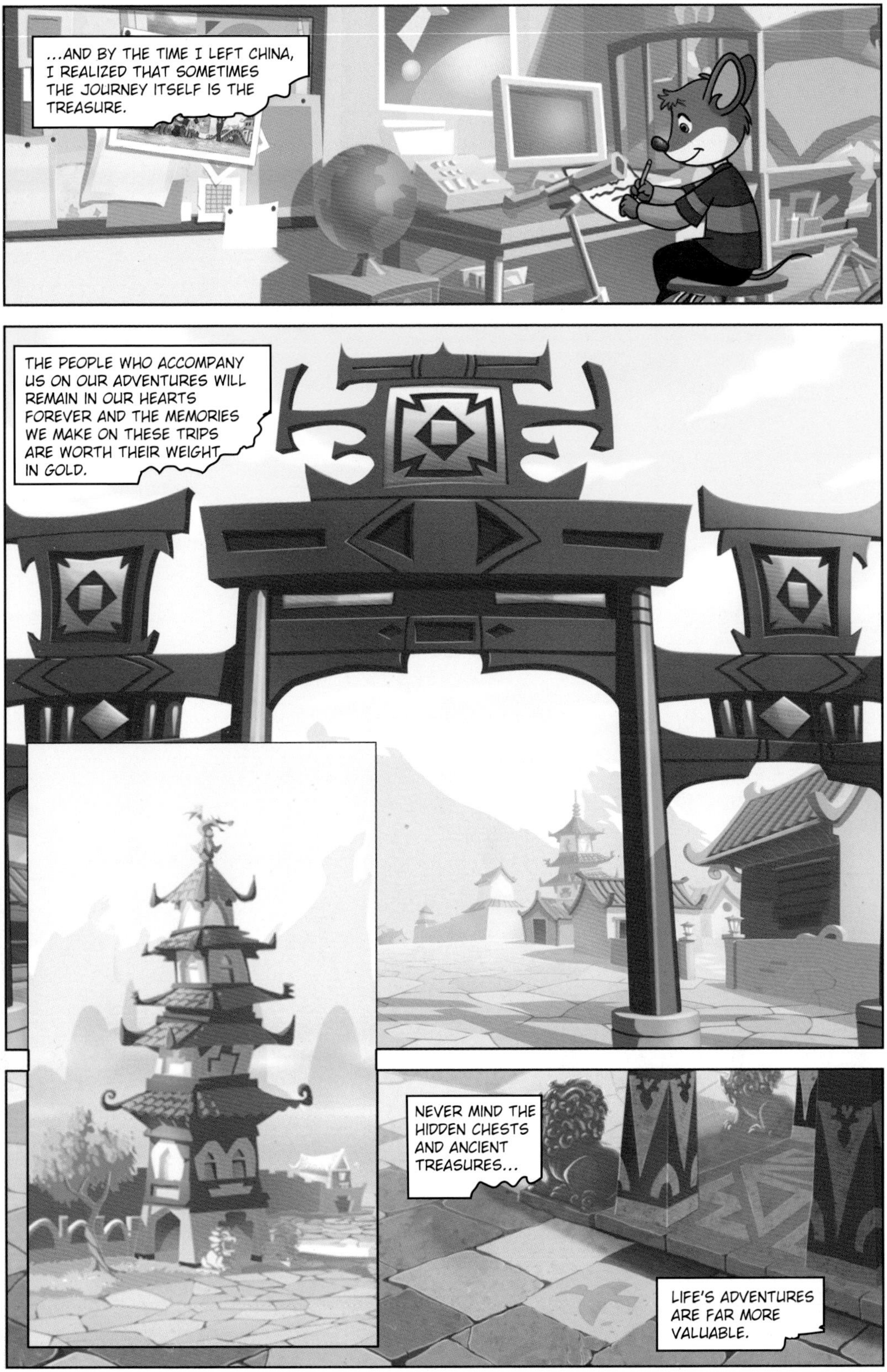
...AND BY THE TIME I LEFT CHINA, I REALIZED THAT SOMETIMES THE JOURNEY ITSELF IS THE TREASURE.
THE PEOPLE WHO ACCOMPANY US ON OUR ADVENTURES WILL REMAIN IN OUR HEARTS FOREVER AND THE MEMORIES WE MAKE ON THESE TRIPS ARE WORTH THEIR WEIGHT IN GOLD.
NEVER MIND THE HIDDEN CHESTS AND ANCIENT TREASURES...
LIFE'S ADVENTURES ARE FAR MORE VALUABLE.

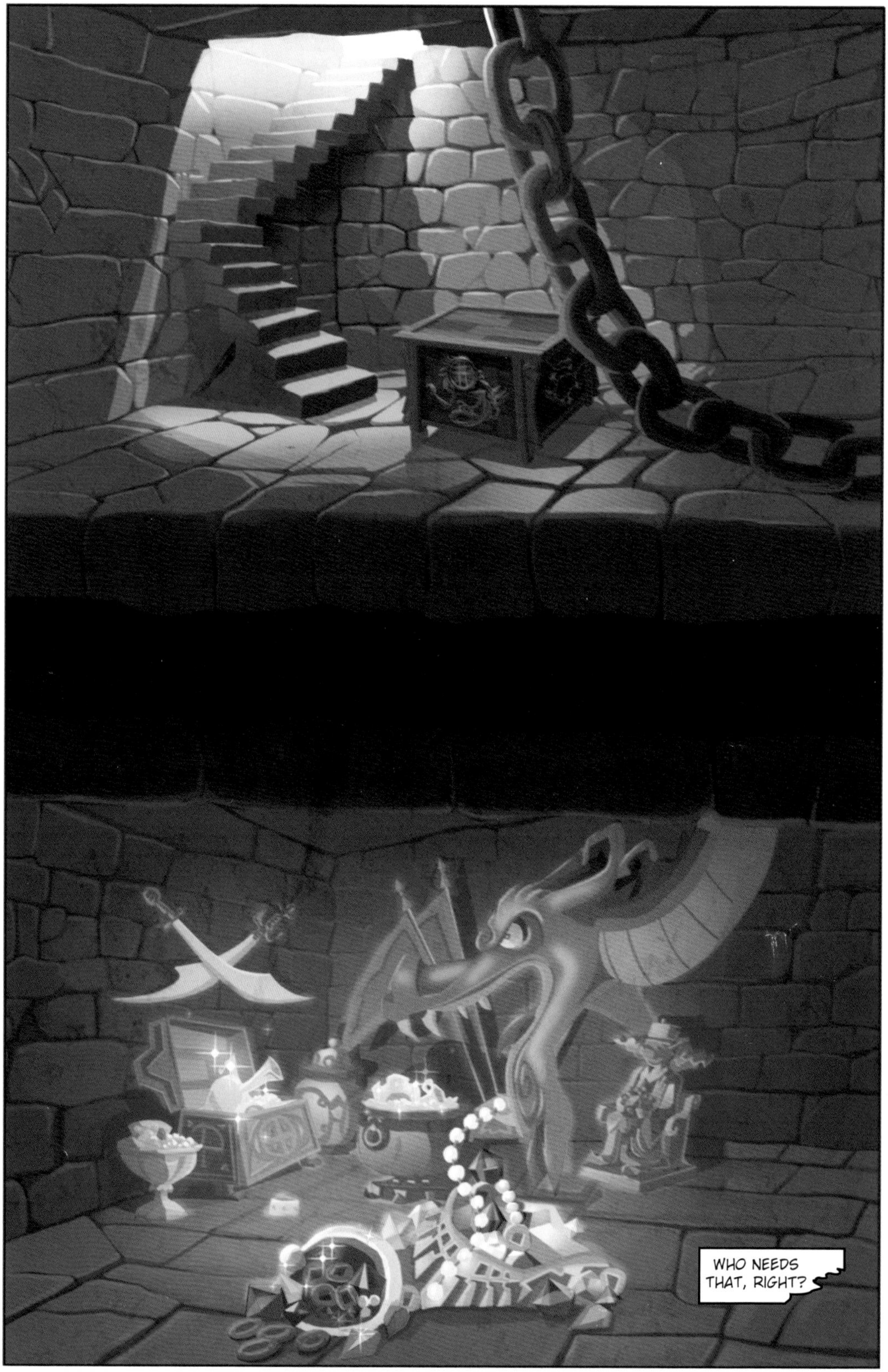
WHO NEEDS THAT, RIGHT?

Watch Out For PAPERCUTZ™

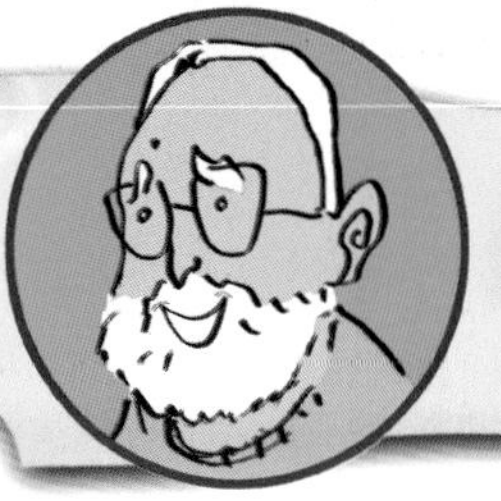

Welcome to the solution-seeking seventh GERONIMO STILTON REPORTER graphic novel, "Going Down to Chinatown," the official comics adaptation of the seventh episode of *Geronimo Stilton*, Season One, written by Laurie Israel & Rachel Ruderman, brought to you by Papercutz—those globetrotting comics connoisseurs dedicated to publishing great graphic novels for all ages. I'm Salicrup, ***Jim Salicrup,*** the Editor-in-Chief and charter subscriber to the *Rodent's Gazette*, here once again with more of *The Philosophy of Geronimo Stilton*. Essentially this philosophy is the guiding principles behind the creation of every Geronimo Stilton story, whether created for books, animation, or comics. You can check out the entire *Philosophy of Geronimo Stilton* online at geronimostilton.com.

But before we get to this installment of *The Philosophy of Geronimo Stilton*, we'd like to mention that "Going Down to Chinatown" was created before the Global Pandemic, and that's why you won't see Geronimo or anyone wearing masks and practicing social distancing by standing six feet apart. We're mentioning this because we wouldn't want anyone to think Geronimo was in any way irresponsible regarding such a serious health threat.

So, now, without further ado, let's examine the next section of the *Philosophy*...

GERONIMO STILTON AND IMAGINATION
The term "imagination" derives from the Latin words "imagination" / "imaginary" (imagine). It is the capacity to visualize things or situations based on the stimulus of everyday life. For example, if you read a book or watch a film, you can imagine you are the protagonist of the book or film. Imagination is a quality that, if used in the right way, can also be very useful to surpass various difficulties and fears like exams, sporting competitions, or public speaking. Imagining yourself in a positive situation helps you to become more trusting and optimistic and leads to the realization of dreams!

We here at Papercutz are lucky that we get to use our collective imaginations every day. Whether we're dreaming up cover ideas for upcoming graphic novels or trying to imagine what new graphic novels we should publish, it always involves using our imagination. And it's not just us—when you see a Papercutz graphic novel's cover in a bookstore or library you use your imagination to picture what the story inside might be like and if you might enjoy it or not. And certainly the writers and artists of other Papercutz graphic novels have to use their imaginations to create fun and exciting stories that you'll enjoy. Using your imagination can feel like magic—for example, if you made up a story and wrote it down, you've created something that didn't exist before. It's really a wonderful feeling when you visualize an idea in your mind and then turn it into something real.
While other Papercutz writers have to use their imagination to come up with stories, good ol' Geronimo Stilton, on the other paw, simply has to report on his latest adventures. But within those adventures he'll often use his imagination to figure out how to solve mysteries or to discover stories to write about for the *Rodent's Gazette*.

But enough talk about imagination, let's wrap up this installment of *Watch Out for Papercutz* with an actual opportunity to use your imagination: What do you imagine the story in GERONIMO STILTON #8, entitled "Hypno-Tick Tock," will be like? To help you out just a little, check out the special preview of that story starting on the next page. We imagine it'll be fun to compare what you imagine to the actual story—which will soon be available from booksellers and libraries everywhere.

Thanks, JIM

STAY IN TOUCH!

EMAIL:	salicrup@papercutz.com
WEB:	papercutz.com
TWITTER:	@papercutzgn
INSTAGRAM:	@papercutzgn
FACEBOOK:	PAPERCUTZGRAPHICNOVELS
SNAIL MAIL:	Papercutz, 160 Broadway, Suite 700, East Wing, New York, NY 10038

Special Preview of GERONIMO STILTON REPORTER Graphic Novel #8 "Hypno-Tick Tock"!

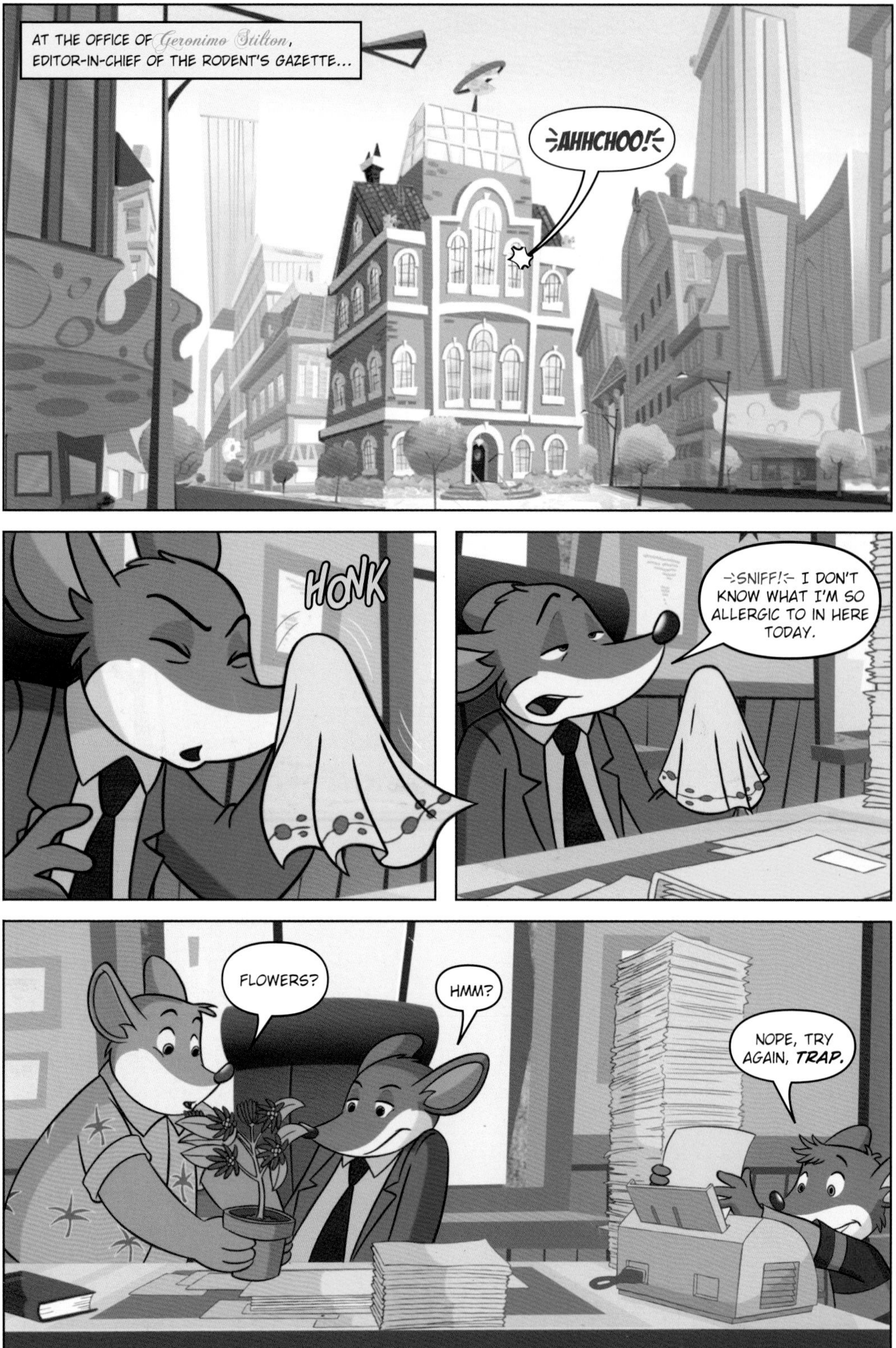
AT THE OFFICE OF Geronimo Stilton, EDITOR-IN-CHIEF OF THE RODENT'S GAZETTE...
AHHCHOO!
HONK
SNIFF! I DON'T KNOW WHAT I'M SO ALLERGIC TO IN HERE TODAY.
FLOWERS?
HMM?
NOPE, TRY AGAIN, TRAP.

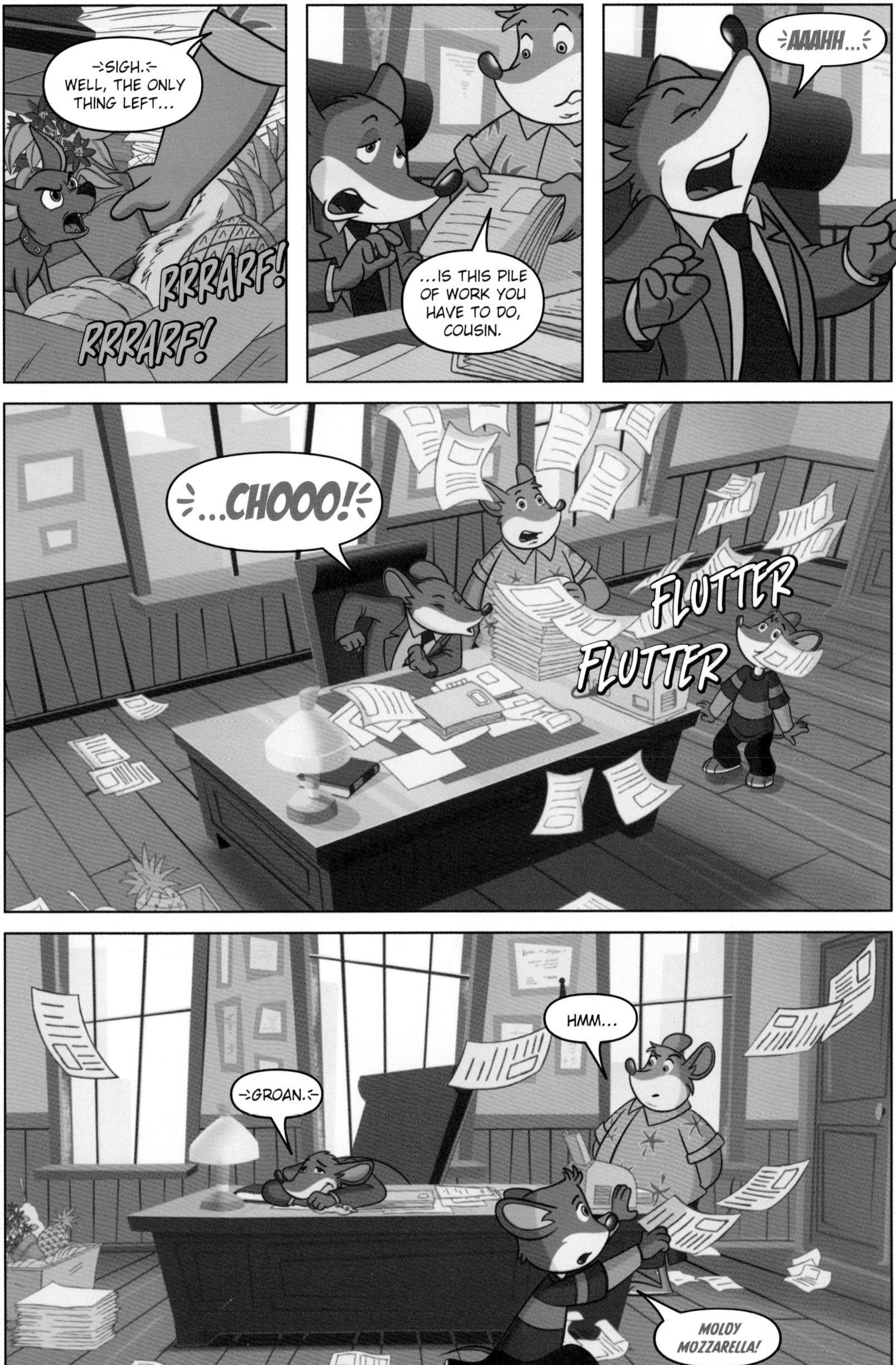
SIGH.
WELL, THE ONLY THING LEFT...
RRRARF!
RRRARF!
...IS THIS PILE OF WORK YOU HAVE TO DO, COUSIN.
AAAHH...
...CHOOO!
FLUTTER
FLUTTER
HMM...
GROAN.
MOLDY MOZZARELLA!

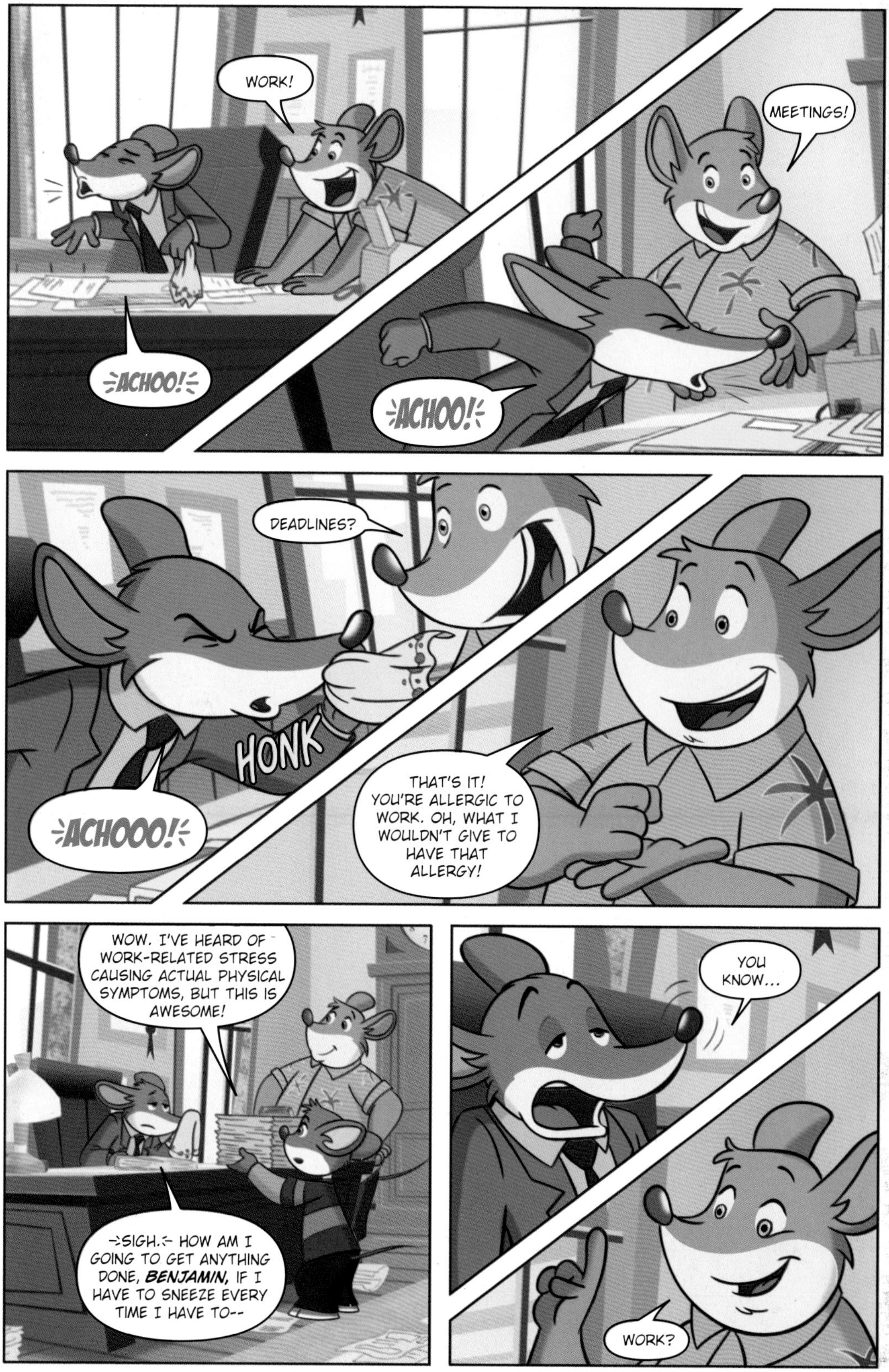
WORK!
ACHOO!
MEETINGS!
ACHOO!
DEADLINES?
HONK
ACHOOO!
THAT'S IT! YOU'RE ALLERGIC TO WORK. OH, WHAT I WOULDN'T GIVE TO HAVE THAT ALLERGY!
WOW. I'VE HEARD OF WORK-RELATED STRESS CAUSING ACTUAL PHYSICAL SYMPTOMS, BUT THIS IS AWESOME!
SIGH. HOW AM I GOING TO GET ANYTHING DONE, **BENJAMIN,** IF I HAVE TO SNEEZE EVERY TIME I HAVE TO--
YOU KNOW...
WORK?

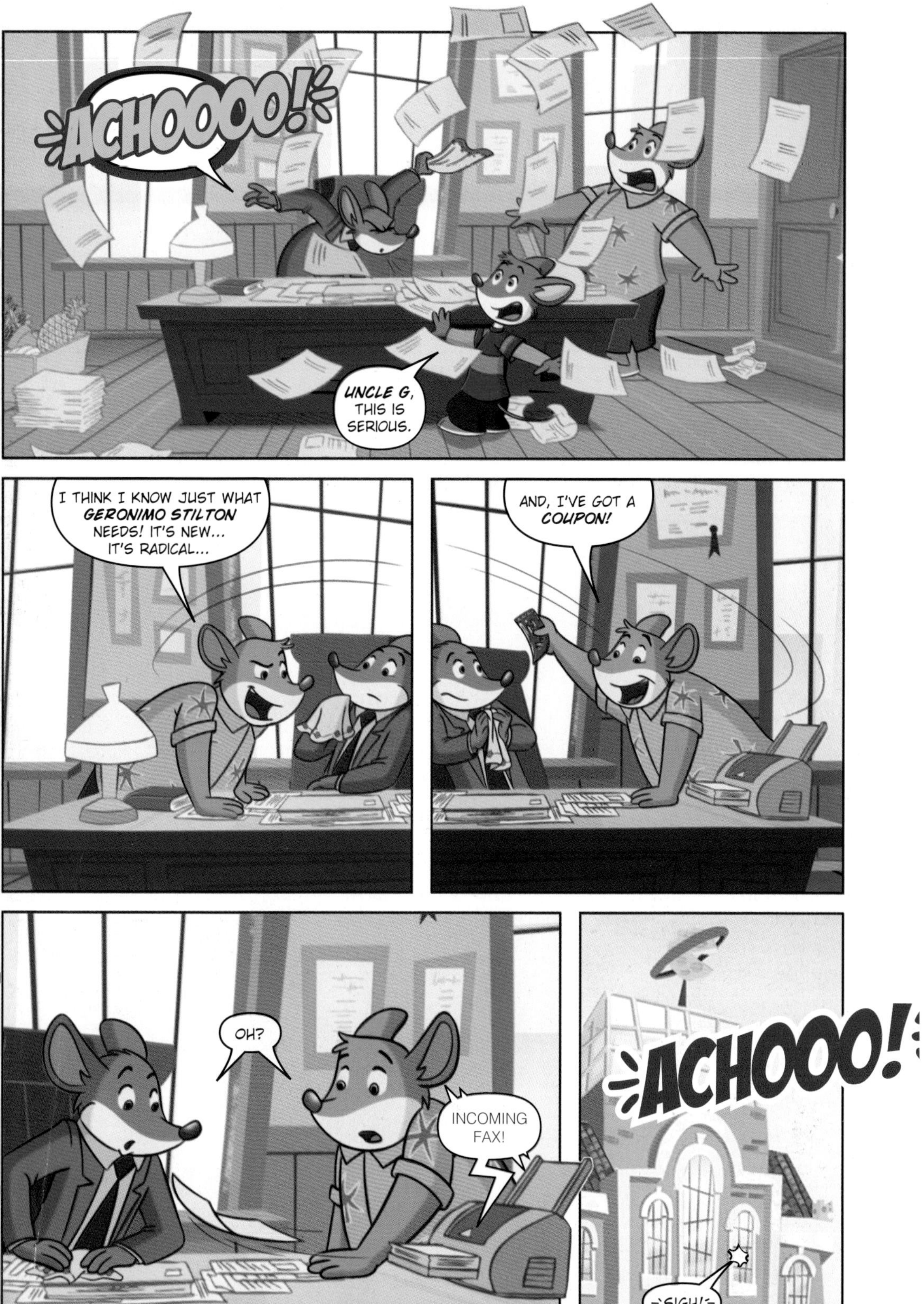
ACHOOOO!
UNCLE G, THIS IS SERIOUS.
I THINK I KNOW JUST WHAT GERONIMO STILTON NEEDS! IT'S NEW... IT'S RADICAL...
AND, I'VE GOT A COUPON!
OH?
INCOMING FAX!
ACHOOO!
SIGH!

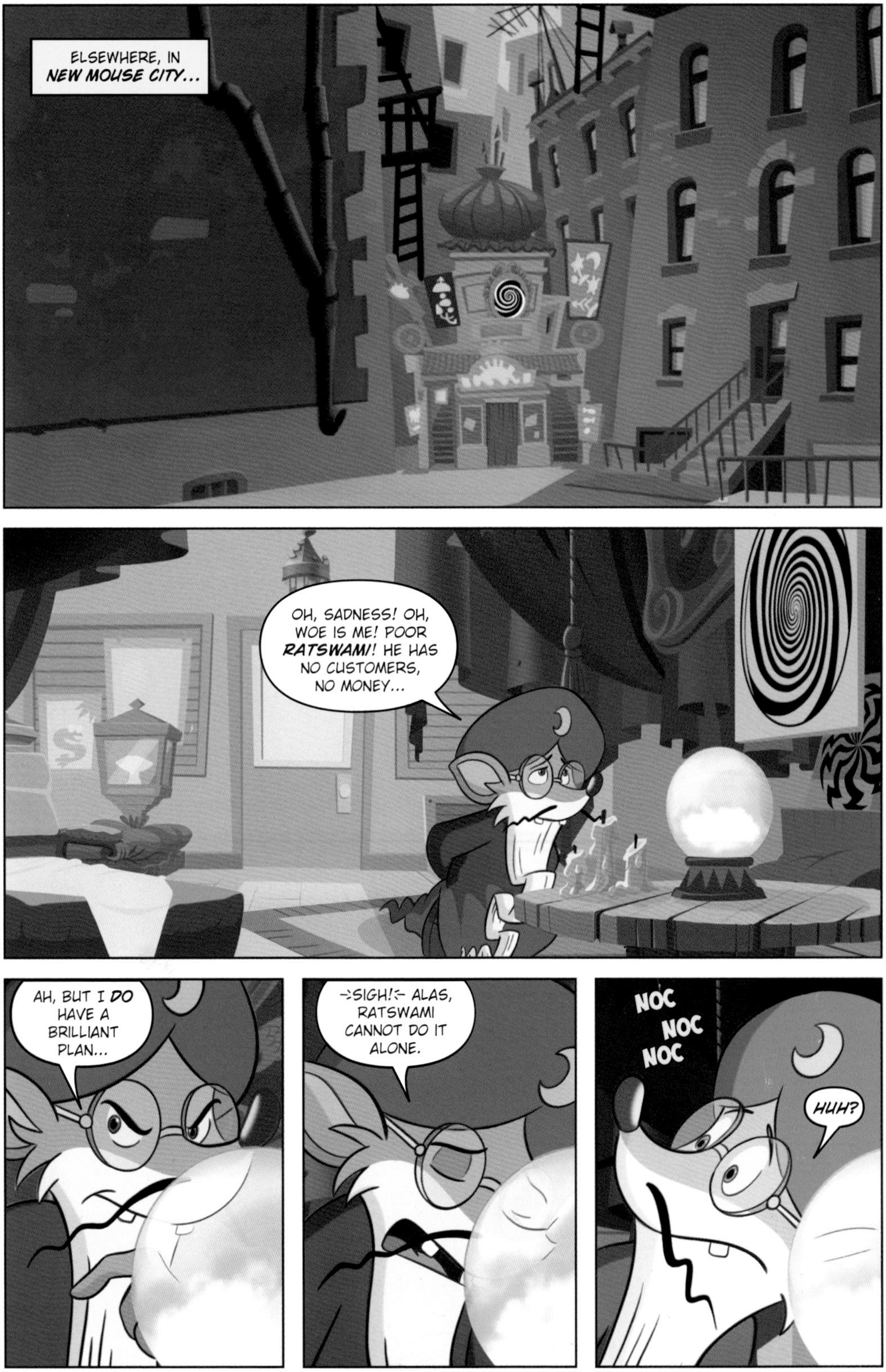
ELSEWHERE, IN NEW MOUSE CITY...
OH, SADNESS! OH, WOE IS ME! POOR RATSWAMI! HE HAS NO CUSTOMERS, NO MONEY...
AH, BUT I DO HAVE A BRILLIANT PLAN...
–›SIGH!‹– ALAS, RATSWAMI CANNOT DO IT ALONE.
NOC NOC NOC
HUH?

Don't Miss GERONIMO STILTON REPORTER #8 "Hypno-Tick Tock"! Coming soon!

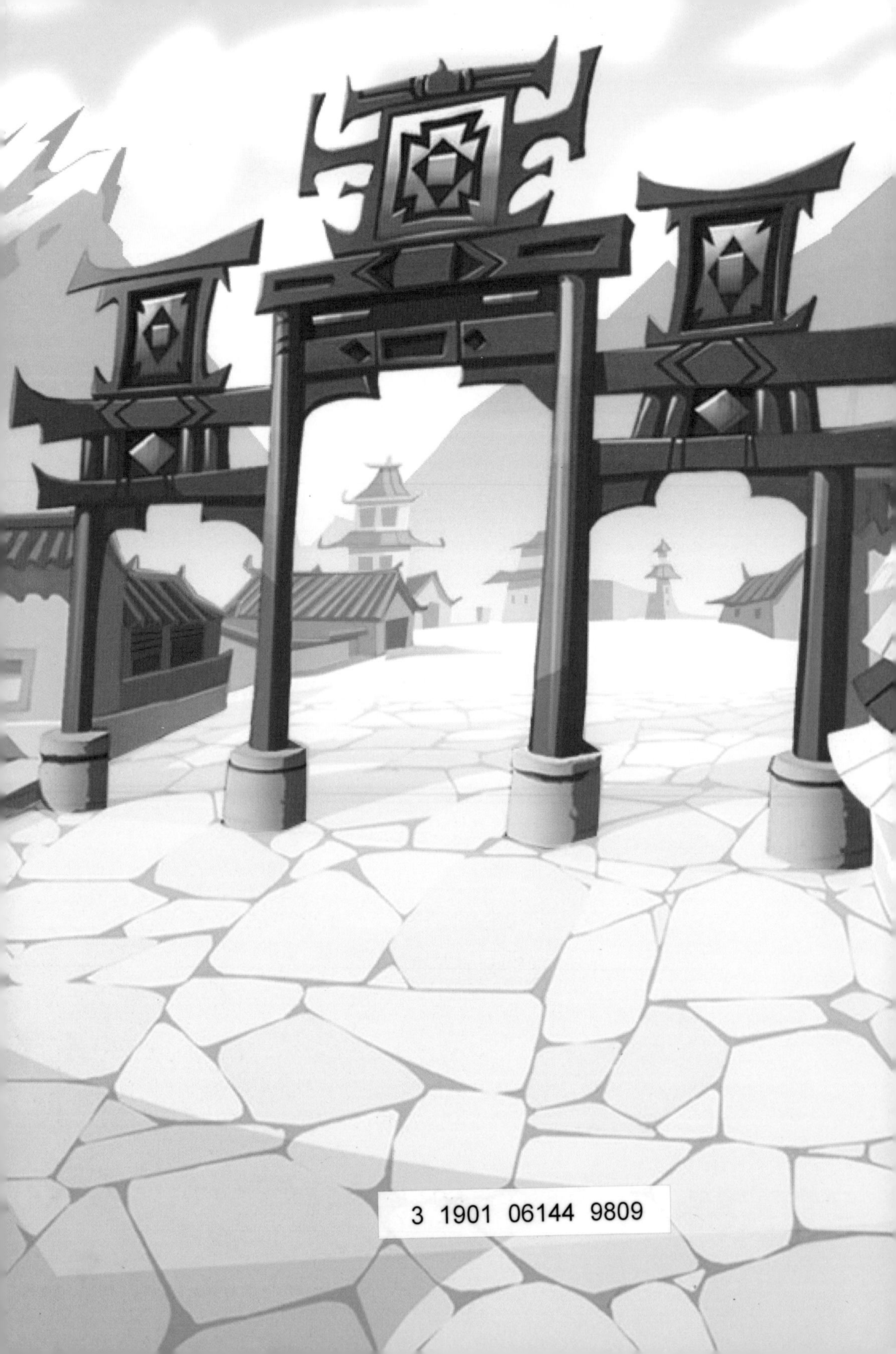